# honeysuckle HOLIDAY

## KATHLEEN M. JACOBS

Jan-Carol
Publishing, Inc

Honeysuckle Holiday
Kathleen M. Jacobs

First Printing Published May 2016
Little Creek Books
Imprint of Jan-Carol Publishing, Inc.
Cover Design: Anna Hartman
Author Photo: Glenn Studio
All rights reserved
Copyright © Kathleen M. Jacobs

ISBN: 978-1-939289-90-2
Library of Congress Control Number: 2016939164

You may contact the publisher:
Jan-Carol Publishing, Inc.
PO Box 701
Johnson City, TN 37605
publisher@jancarolpublishing.com
jancarolpublishing.com

*Dedicated to the memory of my mother,*
*Gloria Ann Bammert.*

*1931–2005*

*I didn't forget.*

*For John*

# honeysuckle
# HOLIDAY

"We wear the mask that grins and lies,
It hides our cheeks and shades our eyes."

From "We Wear the Mask"
Paul Laurence Dunbar


"And he will make thy righteousness to go forth
As the light, And thy justice as the noon-day."

Psalms 37:6


"Laundry is the only thing that should be
separated by color."

Nietzsche

# CHAPTER 1

My sister Lucy still thinks of our father every day. I know this about her
without asking her, even though it has been almost four years since he
was arrested by the Memphis police, as he lay semi-conscious for just
a brief moment on the splintered hardwood floor in the small room we share.
Later he would be charged as an accomplice in the murder of two black, twin,
teenaged boys, who lived ten miles from our house. And as unfathomable as that
truth is, Lucy still finds it hard to believe that our father was so different from who
she thought he was; and yet, that idea—that someone could do something or be
someone completely different from who you thought they were—was an idea that
she continues to encounter again and again as she gets older. It is a part of life, a part
of growing up: the realization that most things are not what they seem.

Four years ago, for instance, she thought our mother non-judgmental, toler-
ant, and stalwart. And she was—in a way; but that changed, too—in a way. And it
was something that for me was apparent early on. How could she not change, after
everything that had happened in her seemingly-perfect world? But it was different
for Lucy. Lucy either didn't see things clearly when they happened or, more likely,
she didn't *want* to see them. Lucy saw things as she wanted them to be, not as they
were, until the clarity was as blinding as the scorching summer sun at noon. There
is something very endearing about that quality, yet it's also very unsettling.

1

Today we say Colored or Negro. And every now and then, we hear someone say black. But four years ago, when we, along with our newly-born baby sister Grace and our mother, left everything familiar to us behind in Germantown and moved to Raleigh without our father, Lucy called them Niggers. So did most everyone we knew. Sometimes I even said it. But whenever I heard someone else say it, I corrected them. And most people vehemently meant it, even if they didn't know what it meant to mean it, what it felt like. But that was before Petey and Lila and Bernie. Before Mark. Before those two sixteen-year-old identical twin boys were murdered. When our father was still Daddy. When he was still alive.

I wonder if Lucy will ever stop thinking about him. I *say* that I have, but that's not entirely true. I mean, how do you completely forget about your father? Is it even possible, no matter what he has done? I don't know. I guess time will tell. But it's been a while now; like an annoying pimple that pops up on my face out of the blue, he still pops into my mind from time to time, even though I try very hard not to think about him. Mama never even allows us to talk about him. It is a mystery to all of us why we would even want to talk about him. And yet, sometimes we do. It just happens. But I have remained staunch in my refusal to say his name. And sometimes Lucy will say something about him, again out of that clear blue sky, without even thinking. Like walking into a dark room and flipping on the light switch, it's reflexive. Like sneezing or hiccupping, it just happens. One minute she might be talking about going for a soda, how much homework she has, or going to see a movie, and the next minute she will bring up something funny Daddy said or something that he and Mama did when they were in high school; then she'll not miss a beat and go right back to talking about whatever it was she was talking about before she brought him into the mix. It's a little unnerving, but we move on.

Sometimes, whenever she journeys into the past and relives that six-month period of her life that changed everything, her gaze fixes on a spot on the faded rose wallpaper in our room. Mama, like a mystic who cajoles you over to her paisley-draped folding table on the state fair midway to read your palm, snaps her fingers in front of Lucy's face. She says, "Lucy Moore, stop that at once!" Lucy closes her eyes, shakes her head, and says, "Sorry." I think sometimes Mama is thinking about him too, and she scolds herself by scolding Lucy.

Last year, when Lucy was hospitalized for ten days with a severe case of food poisoning, she told me that every night when she fell asleep, she heard our father's voice whisper, "Lucy, come here." She would wake with a start, see him at the opened door to her room, "standing as erect as a stored ironing board," and then go right back to sleep. Every time I remember that story, I shiver just a bit. I think it's creepy and scary, even at seventeen years old. Something tells me I'll always think it's creepy and scary, even when I'm eighty. But I hope by the time I'm eighty, I'll have forgotten all about him: what he looks like, his voice, the way he smelled like a blend of citrus and woods. Then again, I sometimes wish he would whisper something to me, too; then I snap out of it, and say a little prayer of gratitude that I've never been awakened by his voice. I don't really want to be, either.

He drifts into her mind whenever she sees a yellow Corvette like the one Daddy used to drive speed past on Stage Road, which happens often since Manny the druggist owns one; whenever she spots a man wearing a starched shirt with his monogram heavily stitched on the pocket or cuff in a deep navy thread; and always, always, whenever someone winks at her. She savors the sweetness of those memories, like the sweetness of the honeysuckle nectar that grows outside our bedroom window, until they are snatched away like a hand from a scalding pot, and she recalls everything from the last Christmas we all spent together as a family to the summer after her twelfth birthday. That brief period of time which seemed to speed by like a flash of lightning, yet lingers slowly like the heat and humidity of a slow, mid-summer southern day, when even the rich luster of the polished magnolia leaves is paralyzed with the heavy weight of a sweltering heat; when the bark of a dehydrated canine seems to travel as slowly as when Grace took her first steps; when freshly-brewed tea melts an entire glass filled with ice before it reaches the rim; when ripples of sweat beads run down your spine, as you anticipate their arrival at your torso. That paradox of time between immediacy and eternity that changes everything. That, for a period of time, erased the eleventh letter of the alphabet from Lucy's lexicon.

No more kites, kittens, kitchens, keys, or kisses. After we found out what Daddy did, she would scream as loud as she could whenever she heard a word that began with the letter k. Lucy screamed like her friend Diane's mother, whose head was always circling and twitching whenever we were outside playing all those summers ago; Diane's mother would scream whenever she saw a wasp. She not only scared the bees away with her screeching and gesticulating, but each one of us jumped a foot off the ground. Mrs. Howell looked ridiculous, of course, but Diane, who was deathly allergic to bees, never got stung.

After Daddy was arrested and Lucy became deathly allergic to the letter k, Mama stood like a sentry at guard to immediately clamp shut the mouth of anyone uttering the word. And Lucy became her apprentice, taking intense precautions herself, readying her palms to cover her ears and closing her eyes tight. Again, it became a reflexive move. And while I think it both troubled and annoyed Mama, it also occupied her time, giving her something to focus on besides what had happened.

When it first began, Mama took Lucy to see Dr. Jewel, who assured her that it was a reaction to what had happened. The doctor told her it was brought about by the trauma of the events. He wasn't sure when, or if, it would ever go away. When Mama told Lucy what Dr. Jewel said, Lucy told her that trauma was just a fancy name for heartbreak. She also assured Mama that Dr. Jewel was wrong, that it would go away in time. And thankfully, her aversion to the letter k didn't last long. Like her aversion to broccoli, once Lila added some melted cheese on top, it wasn't so bad after all.

As time went on, we noticed that every now and then someone would say a word that began with the letter k and it would slip past Lucy. At the moment though, we all looked at each other, held our breaths, and gladly exhaled when it flew over her head.

So, for a time, kittens became felines, kites became darts, and kisses became brushes. Kitchens became galleys, and keys became fobs. She spent a lot of time with the dictionary and the thesaurus. She kept a list of words that began with the letter k in a small spiral notebook that she wore like her favorite pair of jeans. She would spend hours looking up synonyms for words that began with the letter k, then meticulously alphabetize them so that they were readily available. She got to the point where she could recite the list by heart, in a sing-song, like "The Name Game."

When her aversion to the letter k began, my biggest fear was what would happen to Christmas, coffee, cookies, and Coca-Cola, her favorite. When I asked her about these words she said, "Don't worry, Caroline, all I see when I hear those words is the letter c. I don't hear the letter k. It's all about seeing the word." I was happy to hear that, because I had even begun to worry about my own name.

All these things I try to remember about Lucy. There is an urgency to remember them, because in the fall we will move to a different state, one completely surrounded by hills and valleys, and I'll try to keep her from spending too much time in either place. Because when she descends to the depths, she becomes unreachable; when she stretches towards the skies, she floats away before I have the time to grab hold of her ankle and pull her back to me, grounding her once more. I know it will only last for a brief moment in time before she drifts away again, and my prayer—my constant prayer—is that she will always feel those arms around her, even when I am miles away from her. Even when I am gone.

# CHAPTER 2

Lucy's side of the room was, uncharacteristically, rather organized. Her books were arranged neatly in the makeshift bookcase she had constructed from cinder blocks. She had once painted them Coca-Cola red, which had chipped randomly over the years, like fingernail polish shortly after it is applied. At that point in time, it resembled more closely a small Rorschach ink drawing. Neither of us could ever determine if any of those blotches on the cinder blocks might have come from the contact a roller skate made when I hurled it at our father, the night he hid out in the corner of our room, breaking the skin at his temple. We wondered if the blood was forever embedded in one of the tiny crevices of the cinder blocks. Every now and then, when I walked past our bedroom, I found Lucy sitting in front of the bookcase, looking first at the red lettering on one of the Coca-Cola bottles from her collection and then at the chips of old paint on the cinder blocks, the planks of cheap plywood beginning to buckle from the weight of the ever-growing, albeit sparse library. Then she would prick her finger with a needle quickly, enough to draw a drop of blood. Her head moved in rapid succession from the Coca-Cola bottle, to the cinder block, to her finger, as she tried to discern the different hues. Her attention to detail has always been both a gift and, at times, a curse. It drives everyone crazy, but particularly Lucy. She tries to rid herself of the affliction, and is convinced that it is as easy as swatting a fly away—which isn't easy at all, actually. Sometimes she would touch her finger to the cinder block, just to see if the color matched. I once found her with a magnifying glass, examining the three colors of red, like a lab technician looking for comparisons of split genes under a microscope. All she needed was a white lab coat to make it all look official, rather than a little bit crazy. She would look at all three samples, shake her head, put the Coca-Cola bottle back up on the shelf, and suck her finger until it stopped bleeding. It seemed a rather exhaustive process, and yet one from which she gained some measure of satisfaction; afterwards, she would throw herself on the bed and cover her face with her hands, shaking her head until she got dizzy and then she would stop with a sigh of resignation.

Her growing stack of record albums was flush against the corner of the room, and her bed was made. Even the tattered edge of the flower basket quilt, which Aunt Dodo gave her for Christmas the last time we saw her and Uncle Herman, was neatly tucked underneath the mattress and placed at the foot of the bed.

Her small writing table with collapsible legs was centered at the window, which was opened slightly to let in the faint morning breeze, the honeysuckle vine sneaking in to get a peek of what the morning offered.

Lucy's tabletop was as alluring as every outfit worn by Goldie Hawn in *Cactus Flower*, which we had already seen six times. We especially liked the pink ruffled blouse she wore underneath the wine-colored velvet blazer. Who else but Goldie Hawn's character Toni Simmons could get away with pairing a pink, ruffled blouse with a structured, wine-colored velvet blazer? Nobody, that's who. Unless of course it was Goldie Hawn herself.

While my desktop held the essentials—a small yellow lamp with a white shade that Mama trimmed with a navy grosgrain ribbon; a three-ring blue denim binder filled with nondescript, lined notebook paper; and a stack of school textbooks— these things were absent from Lucy's tabletop. Except for the pint-sized, glass milk bottle from Bailey Farms Dairy, which held an array of pens and pencils, there was nothing on my desk that anyone would covet.

Over the years, Lucy had conjured up more trades for that milk bottle, but never proposed anything of any real value that I wanted. She had offered to dry dishes for a week; wash dishes for a week; feed Tina, our German Shepherd, for a week; and pack our school lunches for a week. Never longer than a week, though. Had I made the trade, what would I have had at the end of the week except seven days of dish-free hands, a satisfied dog, and who knew what for lunch, since Lucy's idea of lunch was often a bottle of Coca-Cola and a pack of peanut butter crackers. What I wanted her to offer was a trade for something I wanted that I could hold on to forever, like the sweet little nun doll Aunt Dodo gave her for her tenth birthday, which I truly and probably wrongly coveted; or her collection of Ladybug stickpins that she found attached to sweater sets at Goodwill; ("If you want one," Lucy said, "you have to actually go inside the store and rummage through the stacks of clothes to find them.

There's always at least one every time I go there." But I hated Goodwill almost as much as Aunt Dodo did.); or the black-and-white photograph of Aunt Dodo and Uncle Herman in Arizona, Aunt Dodo holding her multi-colored, beaded handbag that she watched the Indians make on a reservation, hanging at her side; or the long-necked olive green (I simply adore the color green) desk light she kept on the top of her table that arched over everything, with an almost neon glow. All these things were arranged like the chalice, paten, and ciborium on the altar at St. Ann's.

Even the arrangement of Ladybug stickpins beckoned approach. They were lined up in the shape of a cross, on a piece of what was once a deep plum-colored satin ribbon that Lucy had kept from her Easter bonnet when she was five years old. Even though the color had faded over the years to a soft lilac, the ribbon's silky texture seemed to have softened over time, like butter on a piece of freshly-toasted bread sprinkled with cinnamon and sugar.

# CHAPTER 3

Lucy's melodic voice sang along with The 5th Dimension as the lyrics from "Age of Aquarius" seemed to ricochet off the walls throughout our small house, settling eventually on everyone's lips, until we were all singing the hypnotic lyrics of the chorus. Even the sun's rays seemed to chime in as they traveled across our scratched, polished wood floors.

"Lila? Liiilaaa... Lila! Have you finished ironing my shirt yet? You know the one, right? The white one, with the V-neck collar and the red rick-rack trim. The one Mama made for me. Not the one with the Peter Pan collar, which looks too much like my school uniform blouse. Lila, can you hear me? Do you think that looks okay with my plaid capris and penny loafers, or do you think I should wear my pale pink, short-sleeved cardigan with the pearl buttons and little painted flowers on it?"

Lucy was on autopilot, talking so fast it was almost impossible to know where one sentence ended and the next one began.

"Oh, hi Caroline. Didn't know you were in here. Turn up the music. You know how much I love that song."

"Okay, but only because it's your birthday. Don't expect me to keep doing everything you tell me to do once today ends, though." I winked at her, and she stopped just long enough to smile back.

"Oh, you're silly. You know that's not true. Ever since you got accepted at— what's the name of that college? The University of West Virginia or West Virginia University? Anyway, ever since you got accepted at wherever, knowing that we'll be separated, you've acted like we'll never see each other again. Jeez! Mama says it's only a four-hour drive from where we'll be living, so we can come up on weekends, or you can come home. Simple, silly." And she smiled again—that smile that I knew I would miss when it was no longer around every day.

"Lila? Oh, there you are. Sorry."

"My stars, child, what is all the racket about? You would think your party was startin' in the next five minutes. You's got plenty of time, child. But you's got to calm down a bit, sugar. Caroline, you's got to help old Lila out now, you hear? Or else your sister's gonna give me heart palpitations, and I cain't afford none of them."

"Oh, Lila, you know how excited she gets."

"For sure enough, but she's been excited about this here party for near a month now, with all her planning."

"Yes, ma'am. And two months deciding on what to wear. First it was whatever she thought Petey would like to see her in. Then it was what she thought Mama wanted her to wear, and now she's still not sure."

"Oh, hush up, Caroline," and Lucy grabbed the *Seventeen* magazine from my hands.

"Hey, give that back. Lila, did you see what she just did?"

"Now, you two stop acting like a couple of spoilt brats. I done told you about that. It ain't attractive. If'n yous keep this up, I'm gonna have to draw that 'maginary line down the middle of this here room, like I used to do when yous was little girls. Now stop it, I says."

Lucy tossed the magazine back to me, and I said, "I like the pink sweater on you, Lucy."

"Thanks. Me too. What do you think, Lila?"

"Well, I don' rightly think what I think is gonna amount to a hill of beans, but since I done and went and iront this here white shirt for you, like you axed me to this mornin' before I even got through the door, I'd hate to see all that hard work go to waste. Seem like the good Lawd might not like that, either. He don't much like for nothin' to be wasted, I reckon." And then she covered her mouth and snickered.

"Oh, Lila, I don't think there is anything you could ever do that the good Lord would find one bit objectionable," Lucy said, and I chimed in, "Me, neither." Lila brought out her flowered handkerchief that she always kept tucked inside the belt of her navy blue cotton dress and dabbed at her eyes.

"Now, now, chilren, we gots us a party to get ready for, so let's not dilly dally, as your mama would say. Lucy, I likes the pink sweater best too, with that cute pair of blue jeans—the ones you roll up just a bit at the bottom. They looks real nice with your penny loafers. Maybe your mama would let you wear her pearl necklace, to match the pearl buttons on your sweater. Then you can send your picture in to that there magazine. I bet they'd put your picture on the front cover; you's that pretty."

Now it was our turn to wipe away a tear, if only with the gentle glide from the palm of our hands.

"Come on now, chilren, lets us move along," and Lila turned and walked towards the kitchen to check on her fried apple pies, sizzling in the cast iron skillets on every burner of the stove.

I walked over to the record player, lifted the arm gently, and set the needle back down precisely to where The 5th Dimension sang it again and again, reminding us of what we all so clearly needed to hear.

# CHAPTER 4

I t was a small party, but that's what Lucy wanted. And after the past four years, we made sure that she got what she wanted—as much as we could, that is. It was something we gifted to each other, this giving to each other whatever any of us needed at whatever time. Sometimes she wanted to pretend that our father was still alive. She wanted to pretend that he hadn't changed at all—that none of us had. She played this game like a game we used to play when we were younger. Lucy would be the teacher, and I would be her student. We were careful, though, to not let her spend too much time in the world of pretend. We all wanted to pretend that it hadn't happened, but it had. And in our hearts, we knew it all too well. I think that's why she spent so much time with Grace. Sweet little Grace.

Grace was lucky. She had no memory of our daddy, and even though Lucy recalled every minute detail of him, subconsciously she wished she could erase everything she ever knew about him. Like me, there were times she even wanted to forget what he looked like; but every time she looked in the mirror, her high cheekbones wouldn't let her forget. And again, like me, she also wanted to forget his voice; but that probably wouldn't ever happen either, or at least it hadn't happened yet. He'd had a voice so distinct that it slowly crept and coursed into every vein, like the intravenous therapy that Lucy received when she was in the hospital. Drip, drip, drip. It was smooth, and clear, and dreamy, and relaxing—almost hypnotic.

Dr. Jewel told Mama that Lucy sometimes went deep inside herself to both recall and then almost immediately try to forget everything that had happened. "She's in a state of limbo," he said, shortly after it happened. When Mama tried to explain this to her, Lucy said, "Oh, Mama, don't worry. I'm not so sure about Dr. Jewel. I think he got it wrong. But I do like the word limbo. I get it. Like the place you go before you go to Heaven, or God forbid, Hell." Mama assured her that she was not going to go to Hell, but Lucy, like the rest of us, knew all too well that anything was possible. She began to include in her prayers all the suffering souls in purgatory, lighting the candle on her desk that smelled just like the church candles at St. Ann's, musty and sweet at the same time, something she probably picked up at Goodwill. It all makes me shiver just a bit—both the candle's scent and Goodwill.

I watched her like a hawk. My best friend Elizabeth's mother suffered from severe depression, and I wanted to make sure Lucy didn't slip any further away than she had already. Retreating into her own world from time to time was one thing, but to spend day after day crying, like Elizabeth's mother, wrapped up in layer upon layer of coverlets, was quite another. She would go days without showering, eating, or even getting dressed. Lucy, on the other hand, showered sometimes twice a day; changed outfits on the weekend so many times that the floor and the bed became invisible under the mounds of shirts, jeans, skirts, and dresses; and never thought of missing a meal, snack, or even just a taste of whatever Lila was cooking on the stove. Those were the times when I no longer cared as much that she was disorganized and even sloppy at times, or that she seemed to eat anything she wanted and as much as she wanted—Lay's potato chips, Fudgsicles, Hershey chocolate bars with almonds, Lila's fried chicken, and as many fried apple pies as she could eat—without gaining a single pound. Ever. It was exasperating.

Every time I think about Fudgsicles, I remember one summer when we were in St. Louis, visiting Aunt Dodo and Uncle Herman. Mama had a headache, and we went into a place called The Corner Drugstore to pick up some asprin. We had never been there before. And how nondescript is that name? I mean, how much thought does it take to name a corner drugstore The Corner Drugstore? Anyway, when we walked into the store, there was seriously the cutest boy we had ever seen—ever. His name tag read Riley, and even the name was enough to get our attention. We had never known anyone named Riley. And before we knew it, Lucy and I nearly knocked over a display of greeting cards as we continued to keep our eyes focused on Riley. He giggled and winked, and we laughed and turned every shade of red, including shades I couldn't identify. I decided right then and there that I would never go back to The Corner Drug Store—ever.

Later that afternoon, as Mama rested, Lucy found every excuse possible to return to The Corner Drugstore. She needed a pencil and a notebook, even though she never traveled without either one of them. "But I need brand new ones. Mine are all tattered and worn. And I can't seem to find my pencil sharpener, either." Or,

"I must have left my comb at home. I'll just run up to The Corner Drugstore and pick up one. I'll be right back." Or, "Oh, darn, my Bonne Bell lip gloss melted in my purse. I'll only be a minute." Yeah, sure Lucy. Seriously, who did she think she was fooling?

Then, around suppertime, she began to complain of a stomach ache. She got them often, but this time she looked white as a sheet, and the next thing we knew she was making a beeline to the bathroom. Ick. We made an accounting of everything we had eaten that day, but Lucy admitted that she had eaten something that the rest of us hadn't eaten. Fudgsicles. Not one, but three. She didn't buy a new pencil and notebook. She didn't buy a new comb. She didn't buy any Bonne Bell lip gloss. She bought Fudgsicle after Fudgsicle after Fudgsicle. Again, ick. I can barely make it through one Fudgsicle, let alone three in one afternoon. For the longest time after that, every time we walked past a freezer of ice cream bars, Lucy would sprint to the other side of the aisle, closing her eyes and raising a palm against the freezer. As far as I know, she has never eaten another Fudgsicle. And after watching her return again and again to the bathroom and hearing the retching noises, I haven't either. Again, ick.

Lucy is so pretty. She has the longest, skinniest legs of anyone I ever knew (got those from Daddy, too), and deep-set eyes that remind me of the slot in a gum ball machine that seems to bury the coin as soon as you drop it in. Mine seem to just sit flat against my face. But Lucy's are deep, and the color, like her, can change from the deepest blue—almost violet—to the softest green, like four-leaf clovers, which she collects. She keeps them in her wooden Velveeta Cheese box, which she has had for as long as I can remember. The box is also home to her collections of bird feathers, walnut shells, small twigs, tiny acorns, pieces of honeycomb, and butterfly wings, all of which she picks up on her walks in the wooded area around our house. Her long straight, auburn-colored hair seems to ignite when touched by the sun, lighting up even the darkest of days.

Mama had set the table the night before with paper plates, cups, and napkins in navy blue, Lucy's newest favorite color. It was always a shade of blue—sapphire, indigo, cobalt—and for a very long time it was cerulean. Over the years, she had seen all these shades of blue at Manny's Drug Store in Raleigh, lined up in tiny tubes of watercolors. She had become fascinated by the different hues, copying the names down in her notebook, and spent time with each one before moving on to the next.

Elizabeth and I were in charge of playing her favorite songs, beginning with "Born to Be Wild" and continuing, in very specific order, with:

"Sweet Caroline"
"Teach Your Children"
"I Heard It Through the Grapevine"
"Down on the Corner"
"Whole Lotta Love"
"Jumpin' Jack Flash"
"Cloud Nine"
"Magic Bus"
"Suspicious Minds"
"Here Comes the Sun"
"Bridge Over Troubled Water"
"Yesterday"
"Sympathy for the Devil"
"Hey Jude"

and ending, when the cue was given, with number sixteen—sixteen songs for a sixteenth birthday celebration. Like everything else she did, there was a reason for each song and a reason for the order, but she did not share any of them with any of us. Some choices were obvious. For instance, there were days when the only song she played was "Sympathy for The Devil," which was usually whenever she had done or said something to someone that she knew she would end up in trouble over, whenever Mama found out about it (and she always found out about it). Other choices were a mystery, though, and held a place in her heart simply because she liked the message, beat, melody, words, or the story it told. And everybody liked "Magic Bus." At least once a week, as we rode the bus home from school, somebody would start singing that song. Before it was over everybody was singing it, including Cletus, our bus driver.

One day, about a year ago, she was taking a walk through the wooded area behind our house. She said she'd found herself, without even realizing it, in the Armeano twin's front yard, which was littered with everything from old newspapers, to puppies, to feral cats, to flat tires, and old cars propped up on cinder blocks. Mama had warned us to never go anywhere near their place; we had no desire to anyway, since the Armeano twins were two of the meanest, dirtiest boys in town. Anyway, Lucy said that before she knew it, Robby Armeano jumped out in front of her and asked her what the hell she was doing in his yard. Before she could turn and run away, he grabbed her arm, twisted it, and said, "If you show me your thing, I'll show you mine." Lucy said she jerked her arm loose from his so fiercely that she thought she'd pulled a tendon, but she didn't care. She ran so fast down the hill back to our house, Robbie Armeano laughing at her all the way. She tripped and fell right through a patch of poison ivy, and spent the next several days covered in calamine lotion. She played "Sympathy for the Devil" all that day, until I finally took the record off the player. After that incident, she once again returned to the idea of becoming a nun. She thought it might not be such a bad idea, after all. "Nuns," she said, "don't ever seem to get themselves into trouble, don't ever lose their way and wander off to the Armeanos' yard, and don't ever get covered in calamine lotion. And, I'm pretty sure that not a single one of them has ever been asked to show someone their 'thing.'"

The knock at the back door startled us a bit. Lila said, "I got it." Then, "Good morning. May I help you?" "Yes," a young man's voice answered. "I have a delivery for Lucy Moore." "That's fine. I'll take it. Oh my, but they're beautiful." "Just sign here. Thank you, ma'am." "Thank you, young man. I'll see that she gets them."

Lucy and I rushed out of our room and almost knocked Lila over.

The long-stemmed pink roses were arranged perfectly in a clear glass vase, with sprigs of greenery and airy branches of twigs.

"Oh, my," Lucy said as she counted the roses. "Holy cow! Sixteen!"

On the outside of the envelope, centered and neatly typed in all caps, was her name: LUCY. She took the small card from the envelope and breathed in the sweetness of the roses before reading aloud, "Happy Birthday, Sweet Sixteen. You are becoming a beautiful young lady, but you'll always be my little Peanut. Love, Mama, and Mark, too." Then she held the vase of flowers close to her chest, closed her eyes, and sighed melodically. Lila reached for the vase and set it in the center of the table, then propped the card up in front of it.

By the time everything was ready and Mama got home from work, there was no room at all left at the table for anyone to sit down. A plate of Lila's homemade fried apple pies was set at every corner of the table, each one holding a birthday candle. The rest of the table was filled with dishes of homemade macaroni and cheese (Lucy's favorite), crisp fried chicken, sliced tomatoes, creamy coleslaw, and the smoothest, richest brown gravy (Lucy hated chicken gravy. Lila once said that she couldn't have been born in the South and not like white chicken gravy), bowls of shoepeg corn, and cooked, maple sugar glazed baby carrots, drizzled with honey. There were stacks of presents and a festive party hat, which we all knew Lucy would never wear, but Mama would try to get her to anyway—at least for one second, for one picture.

When Mark and Mama walked through the back door, Mama gave Lucy a kiss on the cheek and said, "Lucy, open my present before your party starts." She handed Lucy a small, slender box wrapped in navy paper, with white ribbons and a white bow. Grace was reaching for the box; Lucy gave her the ribbon and the bow to play with, and we all smiled as Grace put the bow on top of her head and wrapped the ribbon around her wrist. As always, she had no idea how happy she made everyone just by being there.

"Oh, Mama," Lucy said, fighting back tears that would surely follow. "Just what I wanted! Just this morning Lila said that maybe you'd let me wear your pearls today, since they would look nice with my sweater. Lila, did you know Mama was going to give these to me?"

"I don't know nuthin'," Lila said, and the tears quickly turned to laughter.

# CHAPTER 5

Petey and Bernie Andrews were the first black students to enroll at St. Ann's Catholic High School when it opened, four years ago. To be precise, they were the first biracial students at our new high school. They moved to Raleigh with their mother, who was white and our religion teacher, and their father, who was our new history teacher. We liked them immediately. Everyone did. I think it was partly because we liked their mother and father, who would wink at each other when they passed each other in the hallways. That small gesture was like the Good Housekeeping Seal of Approval, especially in our family.

Mrs. Andrews was just a bit over five feet tall, thin as a whippet, with short, jet black hair. She wore red, wire-rimmed glasses that hung from a tortoise-like chain around her neck. At her throat hung the tiniest flat gold cross.

Mr. Andrews, however, was as black as midnight and stood over six and half feet tall. His hair was cut close to his scalp and his penny loafers shone as brightly as the pennies they carried. He also wore his glasses on a chain around his neck, but they did not have red rims. He whistled when he was on bus duty, and said, "Peace," as we boarded the steps and took our seats for the ride home.

Petey was a junior like Lucy, and Bernie was a senior like me. They had moved to Memphis from West Virginia, and we were moving to West Virginia at the end of the school year. I guess it was that and Mama saying it was divine intervention that "connected us at the hip" (according to Lila). We were inseparable. Bernie was going to go to West Virginia University, too. Her daddy was trying to see if we could room together, but neither of us had decided if we even wanted to, yet. One minute we were all for it, and the next not so sure. Her daddy just took it upon himself to make a few phone calls and see what he could find out. It was Mrs. Andrews who had to remind him that that wasn't his decision to make. "Now, Pete, you are interfering where you haven't been invited." He said, "You're absolutely right, Ruthie. What was I thinking?" And then they winked at each other, and Bernie and I laughed.

One of the reasons why we were all connected at the hip happened the day Petey and Lucy started to hold hands in the lunch room. At first I thought I was the only one who saw it, until Bernie nudged me in the side. I followed her gaze to their locked fingers, underneath the table. They were smart to keep them hidden, I suppose. I wasn't sure, and I wasn't sure why I wasn't sure.

Then, one day in study hall, Petey was excused to go the bathroom and a few minutes later Lucy asked to be excused. Mr. Andrews turned the corner just as Petey grabbed Lucy to him and touched her cheek with a kiss. Everyone in study hall, including poor old Sister Abigail, who could no longer hear very well nor see very clearly, held their breaths and strained to listen to the voices outside in the hallway.

"Petey! Lucy! What are you doing out of study hall? What are you doing?" Mr. Andrews bellowed.

"I...w-we..." Petey stammered. "Oh shit, Dad, I'm sorry."

"Now, for what are you sorry, son? Using profanity in my presence and in the presence of this young lady, being out of class, or kissing Lucy Moore on the cheek?"

"All of them, sir?"

"I should think so, young man. Now, both of you get back to class at once. And stop whatever it is you're doing. And whatever it is you're doing, we'll talk about it this evening. Before you leave, apologize to me and to Lucy for using a word that I wouldn't have in my hand, much less in my mouth."

"Yes, sir. Sorry, Dad. Sorry, Lucy. I meant no disrespect."

"Fine. Now run along, Petey. Lucy."

"Yes, sir," they said at the same time.

"Holy crap," Petey and Lucy said as they began to laugh, sprinting back to study hall. Just then, the bell rang for us to go to our next classes.

"Holy crap, indeed," Bernie and I said to Lucy and Petey, when they repeated the incident to us on the way home that day. I knew what song would play and replay on the record player as soon as we got back to our house; Bernie knew it too, and began to hum its melody.

Mr. Andrews called Mama that evening, but Lucy had already told her what had happened. It was always smarter to tell on yourself, especially when you knew you were going to be found out, and probably before you could tell the story yourself.

"When I was a young girl," Mama began, after Lucy told her what had happened, "there was a saying. 'Tell me who you go with and I'll tell you what you are.'"

"Mama! That's horrible!"

"Hold on, Lucy. I didn't say I like the saying or that I agree with it, but I wanted you to know it."

"Why?"

"Because no matter what has happened before, what is happening now, or what is yet to happen, mixing the races will be something that most people won't like. Most people will not ever accept it."

"But that's wrong, Mama."

"I know it is, Peanut, but it's also true. Before I met your daddy, I worked as a bank teller."

"I didn't know that."

"Well, I did. I also had an apartment downtown, across the street from First National. Anyway, there was another teller there who, like Mrs. Andrews, was white and was married to a black man. They also had two children, a boy and a girl. They had no friends, and no one in either of their families would ever talk with them or see them. They were a very quiet family, and often alone. When you saw them all together, though, I remember thinking that they looked like a very happy family. The parents were always telling jokes, and the children were always laughing. But I thought about what a hard life they must live, to be looked at by others as different, less than normal, whatever that is."

"I like Petey, Lucy, and Caroline and Bernie have lots of fun together, but it is still something that even ten or twenty years from now will never be accepted, not by everyone. I don't like it, but it's the truth."

Lucy kept her head down through most of the conversation, sniffled, and pushed back her cuticles, as she often did when she was nervous, scared, or both. Then she said, "Okay," and got up and walked away. Mama reached out for her, but Lucy didn't see that. Then Mama got up, walked into her bedroom, and began to slip out of her work clothes and into something more comfortable.

# CHAPTER 6

Petey handed Lucy the prettiest wrapped present that any of us had ever seen. It was almost too pretty to open, but both of them were too excited to waste any time in unwrapping the shiny silver paper and the navy satin ribbon. Lucy guessed that it was a book, but she had no idea that it would be a signed, first edition of *To Kill a Mockingbird* that had belonged to his mother. Lucy nearly fainted, holding the treasure next to her heart and kissing Petey on his lips without caring one little bit who saw her. Everyone did, and both surprisingly and thankfully, no one said a word.

Bernie and I went in together with Elizabeth and Diane, pooled our finances, and got her a bottle of Chanel No. 5 *perfume*, not cologne. She immediately broke the black seal and dabbed some strands at the back of her hair. We all admitted that it was, by far, the most divine scent ever created—even Mark and Petey had to agree.

The last gift to be unwrapped came after we all sang "Happy Birthday" and helped Lucy blow out all sixteen candles, on all sixteen fried apple pies. It was from Lila, and it was her very own childhood nun doll that she had painted with black paint so that her face would no longer be white. We all cried, and I couldn't help but covet that one, too.

Lucy looked at me to signal that it was time. She walked to our room and brought out a framed black-and-white photograph of our father. It was taken in our back yard in Germantown, at Easter 1960. We were each dressed in our frilly Easter dresses and bonnets. We both held a white patent leather purse in one hand and an Easter basket in the other, our matching white patent leather Mary Janes gleaming like mirrors. Daddy was crouched between us, an arm around each of our waists, wearing a smile that could melt any girl's heart. Crocuses, tulips, blossoming Bradford pears, and pink dogwoods created a canopy that looked like a row of opened umbrellas behind us. Next to that photo, Lucy placed a small plastic frame that held a yellowed newspaper clipping with a photograph of two twin, sixteen-year-old black boys, their names penciled in below their picture. I placed the needle at the beginning of the song and Lucy said, "A toast. To Thomas and Albert and Daddy." And after everyone touched their party cups in silence, we all, as if rehearsed, said, "Peace," while "Let It Be" echoed throughout the house. Mark's and Mama's eyes were as big as the top of their party cups; they didn't say a word, giving Lucy what she wanted.

# CHAPTER 7

One week after Lucy celebrated her sixteenth birthday, Lila turned sixty. Several years ago, when Lucy discovered that Lila's birthday was one week after her birthday, she decided that it was all part of a bigger plan. This plan was being orchestrated by someone other than herself, forcing her, whether she liked it or not, to look at what was happening around her. It was like something that keeps appearing over and over that you keep tripping on every time, thinking the next time it happens you will be able to avoid it, simply by knowing you are going to run into it again. Kind of like Grace's toys; every time you turn a corner, you trip on one. While it might be annoying, it is also reassuring. It's sort of comforting, knowing that sweet, little Grace is always there. Something the nuns and Mama often referred to as divine intervention. They would often say it might not be easy to define, but you would know it when it happened to you. You could try to ignore it, but it would never go away. And once you knew it, you were glad that you hadn't ignored it. Instead of kicking the toy out of the way, you simply picked it up and put it in the toy box.

Lila had been a member of our family for over four years, and while Lucy had grown to love her like we all had, it wasn't always that way—at least not for Lucy. Over the past several weeks, particularly, she had been trying to figure out what we could get her as a family, not just individually. It was important to her that the gift be a family gift. Every time we asked Lila what she would like for her birthday, she said that being a part of our family was enough. Since both of her parents were no longer living and she had never married or had children of her own, God had given her our little family to mother, she would tell us. Whenever she said this, and she

22

said it many times over the years, we would all smile at her and feel bad that we had ever said anything mean to her, especially Lucy.

"I want to do something really special for her," Lucy said. "But, I can't think of a darn thing."

"Don't worry," I said. "We'll come up with something."

"But what?" she would persist, rather annoyingly, I might add.

"Well," I suggested, "she loves to read and likes nice books. We've given her books before, and she always likes them. We could all sign our names and write a little message to her."

"Yeah, but I want to give her something that we've never given her before. It's her sixtieth birthday, and it has to be something really special. Like my sixteenth birthday. Your sixtieth birthday is that special, too. And whatever it is, we need to think of it fast. I mean her birthday is the twenty-fourth, which is next Tuesday. Less than a week away. Holy cow! We have to think of something fast, Caroline."

We had all been to Lila's house. It was sparsely decorated, with a single dark brown velvet couch, two end tables, two table lamps, a kitchen table and chairs, and a bedroom suite. Much like ours, come to think of it. She had a small bookcase filled with history books and Louis L'Amour westerns, which we all found kind of odd, but never said so. Mama would have smacked us silly if we had. She had a colored picture of Jesus in a simple frame on the wall, alongside a framed picture of her mama and daddy on their wedding day. She had a small TV that sat on a table with casters. All the curtains in her house matched. The same ones were in the living room, the dining room, the bedroom and the kitchen. They were red and white checked, without a single wrinkle in any of them. Her bed was covered with a solid red quilt, and a single toss pillow was centered between the two bed pillows. It had praying hands appliquéed on it in lots of colors and the words "PRAISE JESUS" stitched above them in gold thread. She'd told us it had been her mama's, and that she treasured it more than anything else she had. In addition to all of her window curtains matching, every rug in every room matched, too. They were all solid white, and spotless. We wondered how she managed that, but then again we didn't ask. It was both nondescript and incredibly beautiful. An enigma, I suppose. She had a small dressing table in her bedroom, too, neatly arranged with her white comb, a bottle of Tabu, a small flowered trinket tray holding some earrings, an oval-shaped silver mirror, a nail file, a bottle of red nail polish, and a pot of rouge. In the center, there was a framed photograph of our family that she had asked Mama for last Christmas. She said, "It's the only thing I wants, Miz Maggie," when

Mama asked her what she wanted for Christmas. We got her other things over the years, of course: nightgowns, slippers, books, a handbag, and a red sweater. But the only thing she ever told Mama she wanted was a picture of our family. There was something about seeing that framed photograph on her dressing table that made me happy. I think it might have been the fact that someone else loved us, besides family. It was a simple notion, but one that made me smile every time I thought about it—that even across town, someone else was looking out for us.

Lucy was sitting at the kitchen table reading the morning paper, when she suddenly shouted my name.

"You don't have to shout, Lucy, I'm right here."

"This is it. And it's perfect."

Lucy folded back the paper, smoothed it down, and said, "She'll love it!"

"What is it? And why is it perfect, whatever it is?"

"Listen," she said.

"First of all, what's the date? Today. What's the date today?"

"I don't know. Why?"

"I need to know, that's why."

"Well, for heaven's sake Lucy, check the paper."

"Oh, yeah. Okay."

Lucy looked at the top of the page she was reading from and said, "It's the nineteenth. Holy cow! We don't have much time to plan."

"Plan what? What did you find?"

And Lucy began to read the article to me.

"A documentary titled *King: A Filmed Record... Montgomery to Memphis*, which combines newsreel footage, footage of Dr. King's famous speeches, and many on-screen commentaries by celebrities such as Paul Newman, Joanne Woodward, Ruby Dee, and James Earl Jones will be shown on Tuesday, March twenty-fourth as a one-time-only event, in select theaters across the country. Tickets are five dollars each. The purpose of the screening is to raise money for the Dr. Martin Luther King, Jr. Memorial Fund. The film includes King's famous 'I Have a Dream' speech and his final speech, 'I Have Been to the Mountaintop.' The film documents the life and work of Dr. King from 1955 to 1968."

"You're right, Lucy. That *is* the perfect gift. She will love it!"

One week later, after we had all seen the documentary, everyone left the theater without saying a word. Everyone. The theater was packed, and people were crying, including all of us. Mama and Mark went with us, of course, and so did the Andrews family and Elizabeth and Diane. Mama had made plans for Grace to stay the night with her friend Mary. But after we left the theater, Mama went straight to Mary's and picked up Grace. She wanted her with us.

In the documentary, Dr. King said he was tired of evil and hate, and that he would never resort to violence. The film showed reactions towards blacks when they would enter restaurants, the violence of the KKK, and attacks on black churches. And yet, King continued to preach for peace. The worst shots were those that showed gas being shot out at blacks and water being shot at them from fire departments' hoses. And the screams coming from black men, women, and children will forever ring in our ears. It was deafening. But it was the eulogy delivered by Joanne Woodward for the four young girls killed by dynamite ignited by white supremacists in Birmingham in 1963 on their way to Sunday school that not only dealt the most powerful blow, but also made each of us bow our heads in shame.

As we left the theater, Lila walked between us, and we each reached for one of her hands, holding on until she lightly squeezed it, letting us know that we weren't to blame.

As we drove her home, the silence in the car was broken when she began to hum "Amazing Grace," eventually breaking into song until we all joined in, Lila helping us recall the words that we stumbled over or simply forgot.

I couldn't help but remember the reading from mass two days before, from Isaiah: "and a little child shall lead them." I said a short prayer for those four little colored girls who were killed in Birmingham: Addie, Cynthia, Carol, and Carole. Names so close to mine. And like Grace, they were sweet little girls. They were what Dr. King knew to be our hope—our only hope. And suddenly, like Mama, I was in a near panic to see Grace.

LUCY
WINTER, 1965

# CHAPTER 8

When Daddy left on Christmas Day, he didn't take anything with him. He just walked out the front door and down the street, his hands in the pockets of his wool camel-colored trousers. He pulled his white shirt collar up, a slight protection against the strong wind. Caroline and I were on the sofa on our knees, watching through the plantation shutters. As he reached up to his collar, I could see the navy monogram on his French cuffs. We watched, craning our necks, until we could no longer see him. He never turned back, not even when we knocked on the window to get his attention. We kept waiting, hoping he would turn around and wave, then Caroline and I would join in, continuing until we couldn't see each other anymore. It was a family tradition when someone left to wave until they were out of view. It was a sign that they would see ya later. But Daddy never turned around, and something told us to not go after him. I don't know what that something was, but it could have had something to do with Mama's indifference. *She* wasn't going after him. We turned to look at Mama, who held Grace close to her; Grace's cooing drew us away from the window, like a mourning dove's nighttime coo.

Grace was only six weeks old. She was so tiny and cute in her white smocked jumper, with little red stitched reindeer galloping through a forest of evergreens.

"Well, now. What shall we do on this fine Christmas morning?" Mama asked. She straightened her shoulders, held her head high, and brushed back a fallen curl from her eyes, like there was nothing unusual about the day.

Caroline and I looked at each other in puzzlement and shrugged our shoulders. "Mama?"

"Yes, my little Peanut?"

"Where is Daddy..."

"We'll talk later," she said before I could finish my sentence. "Right now, how about some French toast and bacon?"

Caroline and I loved Mama's French toast. It was always perfect, with the maple syrup warmed, a dusting of powdered sugar on top, the butter pat slowly melting over the sides, and never, never getting close to the crisp bacon. We always wondered how she did that. The orange slice and strawberry on the side of the plate were like colorful ornaments on our Fraser fir tree.

"Okay," we said.

Mama went to the kitchen and we hurried in after her, afraid that she, too, might disappear. Grace's carriage was in front of the window seat, the bright early morning sun moving across it like a fairy sprinkling a light dusting of happiness from her wand. Mama laid her gently inside, the white cashmere blanket that was a gift from Aunt Dodo and Uncle Herman placed weightlessly over her little body.

While I was anticipating Mama's warm French toast, I couldn't stop the questions from gathering like a fierce wind in my head. *Did Mama know Daddy was leaving? Why is she so calm? Is she scared? Will he be back? Maybe he just went for a walk. If not, where did he go? Why did Mama flinch? Why didn't he take anything with him?* And then, just like coming out of a hypnotic state, the questions were replaced by the delectable scents coming from French toast sizzling, bacon crackling, and warm maple syrup slowly dripping from the spout.

Mama already had the table set, the white linen napkins monogrammed in red sitting on top of each gold-rimmed plate, looking as if they might rise up and float about the room like bubbles blown from a plastic wand. Mama began to sing. "We wish you a Merry Christmas, we wish you a Merry Christmas, we wish you a Merry Christmas, and a Happy New Year."

"Jingle bells, jingle bells, jingle all the way. Oh, what fun it is to ride in a one-horse open sleigh. Hey! Jingle bells, jingle bells, jingle all the way, oh what fun it is to ride in a one-horse open sleigh." Caroline smiled at Mama.

27

"Jolly ole St. Nicholas, lend your ear this way. Don't you tell a single soul what I'm going to say. Christmas Eve is coming soon, now you dear old man. Listen..."

"Oh rats! I can't remember the rest," I said. Then we all laughed.

Caroline and I always tried to get the orange off the rind without breaking the rind. It was a kind of a contest, and one that Caroline always won.

Mama had carefully gathered up Grace, like a delicate loaf of bread. Grace looked up at Mama as she fed her the bottle of milk. Every now and then, Mama took the corner of the bib, embroidered with "Baby's First Christmas," and dabbed at Grace's little mouth.

"I was thinking, how would you like to ride the train and go to St. Louis?"

"Oh, my gosh!" I said. If there was anything that could get my mind off of what had just happened, it was the thought of taking the train to St. Louis; although we had done so many times, I had never grown tired of it.

Caroline, who seldom got excited about much of anything, scooted back her chair, danced around the kitchen, and said, "Absolutely!"

"Well, then. Let's get packed."

Caroline and I ran upstairs and opened the drawers like a couple of monkeys, throwing our clothes inside the suitcases. Now that wasn't so unusual for me, but Caroline was the neatest person I'd ever met. Yet even she didn't care if the clothes were wrinkled by the time we got to Aunt Dodo and Uncle Herman's house. We didn't even grab our toothbrushes, knowing Aunt Dodo would have extras.

We shouted, "We're ready!"

We nearly tripped going down the stairs, the suitcases dragging behind us, clomp, clomp, clomping down each step.

"Lucy, grab a book," Caroline said. We scrambled under the Christmas tree, shoving aside wrappings and presents.

"Found it!" Caroline exclaimed.

"Found it!" I mimicked.

Pine needles fell from the branches as we scurried off, *The Secret of the Old Clock* and *A Tree Grows in Brooklyn* secure under our left arms. Mama was already at the door, her suitcase beside her. Another question: *how did she pack so quickly? I'll think about that later.* Grace was bundled up, Mama had her navy coat buttoned, and Caroline and I threw our new mufflers about our necks, the fringe ready to fly.

When we all reached the front door, Mama moved her head slowly to look around the room. Her eyes touched for the briefest of moments on the baby grand piano; the built-in book shelves, filled to overflowing; the floor-to-ceiling silk taffeta draperies in shades of moss and cream, with slender evergreen trees embroidered down the sides; her writing table, stocked with neat stacks of engraved stationery; the plush white carpeting; and the stacked-stone fireplace. Then she closed her eyes, put her head back, and breathed in and exhaled with such certainty that Caroline and I followed suit, although we didn't know why. Then she said, "If there was one thing you could take with you, knowing that you might never return, what would it be?"

Caroline and I stared incredulously at each other, and Mama said, "Well, come on, pretend."

"That's easy," said Caroline. "My books."

"Me, too," I echoed. And then quickly added, "And if I could add one more thing, it would be one Barbie doll."

"Okay, then," Mama said. "Caroline, go get another suitcase from the basement. Lucy, you go with her. Pack as many of the books as you can and squeeze in as many Barbie dolls as will fit, and hurry back as soon as you can."

We filled the suitcase with as many books as we could and tucked the Barbie dolls inside the compartments; in a panic, I grabbed my little nun doll, squeezing her into a little open slot at the front of the suitcase. And right before we turned to leave, I scooped up my wooden Velveeta Cheese box and tucked it under my arm.

We worked as excitedly as the time when we were kids and played musical chairs at the school carnival, afraid that we'd be left out when the music stopped. We didn't know how much time we had to gather our most prized possessions before Mama called us back downstairs. Once we filled every crevice of the suitcase, Caroline stopped and looked around her room with the same resignation that she saw Mama do downstairs. She looked at me, nodded her head, picked up the suitcase with one hand and took hold of mine with the other, and we began our descent.

# CHAPTER 9

Ten minutes before the train pulled into Union Station, Mama said, "Comb your hair, we're almost there." Caroline and I said, "Yes, ma'am, conductor Sam." For as long as I can remember, we chanted this rhyme right before the train arrived in St. Louis.

Aunt Dodo and Uncle Herman were always waiting excitedly for us right inside the station. Caroline and I ran past the rows of polished benches and into their outstretched, welcoming arms. The mix of Emeraude, cedar shavings, and Uncle Herman's Camel cigarettes was sweet, reassuring, and familiar. "Maggie," they beckoned, waving wildly, as we burrowed our faces in the folds of their soft winter coats.

Mama handed Grace to Aunt Dodo, who kissed her little cheeks, eyes, and tiny nose. "You are the cutest little baby in the entire world. Even cuter than the Gerber baby. Yes, you are." Uncle Herman's arm was around Mama's shoulders, her head resting gently on his black cashmere overcoat. She shuddered from the cold, and he whispered, "Everything's going to be fine." He reached inside his pocket and handed her a starched, white linen handkerchief with his monogram, HJR, in bold black thread, and she dabbed at her eyes.

"Bundle up, little ones. It's cold outside," Uncle Herman said.

The snow was falling in big, fat flakes. Caroline and I opened our mouths, stuck out our tongues, and caught as many as we could, fearing that it would soon stop snowing, and we wouldn't ever again be able to taste the ice particles that settled onto our tongues.

"Hurry, now, let's get in the car. Clementine's is waiting."

Clementine's was one of our most favorite places in the universe. They served juicy steaks, crispy steak fries, and beefsteak tomatoes. Caroline and I loved the word steak; it had such a definite punch to it that it was near profanity, except it didn't fit into the four-letter category.

Last year in English class, Sister Mary Michael spent a whole week talking about acrostic poems. I was bored silly, to say the least, until she told us to write one. And, if she chose to put it on the chalkboard, we wouldn't have any homework that night. Suddenly we *all* came to attention. We were all game. Mine was titled "Steak & Eggs." And the next morning, it was written on the chalkboard. At first I was a bit mortified, but as everyone soon reminded me, I was their savior—at least for one night.

"Steak & Eggs"
Simply
Tasty,
Elegant,
And
Knowingly scrumptious and, at times, quite piquant.
Even
Great
Grubs like steak & eggs
Sing beautiful songs.

I still have no idea where I got the last line, but Sister liked the poem, because I had used two new vocabulary words from our weekly vocabulary list and I had sketched a juicy filet and a fried egg underneath my name. She also wrote at the bottom of my paper, "There is something about the last line that makes me happy. I'm not quite sure why I like it, but one reason could be that it took me by surprise, and that's what a poem is supposed to do. Good job." I beamed.

As Uncle Herman steered his brand new, black, shiny Buick along Gravois Avenue, I spotted the bright orange and green neon sign announcing Clementine's Fine Food, like a carnival ride along the midway at the state fairgrounds. It was mesmerizing, and Caroline and I edged to the front of our seats, faces pasted to the windows, anxious to jump out of the car and run to get there before anyone else could.

Jake Clementine was about 5' tall, skinny and bald. He was always impeccably dressed in a black wool suit, starched white shirt, and a purple bow tie with floating white feathers on it. I wanted to slip his tie from around his neck, toss it up in the air, and see if those feathers would float. Like my daddy, he wore his monogram—JPC—on his French cuffs, worked in a deep plum thread. His teeth gleamed when he smiled; Mama said she didn't think they were real, but we were to never, ever say such a thing to Mr. Clementine. He wore a perfectly-folded, starched white linen breast pocket square with a simple C embroidered on it in the same deep plum thread. His gold belt buckle shone brightly with any slight movement.

He owned hundreds of antique and modern cufflinks. Seriously, hundreds. That night, he had on my favorite pair: antique Chihuahua diamond and ruby cufflinks that he bought at an antiques shop in Paris. KMOX-TV once ran a special feature on Mr. Clementine, showcasing his collection of antique cufflinks, his Chihuahua Coco barking at the end of the segment.

Mr. Clementine never goes anywhere without Coco, who "barked and barked and barked when she saw the cufflinks," Mr. Clementine said, until he just had to purchase them, and then she smiled—that's what he said, anyway—and took a nap. He wore dark silk socks and a pair of magnificent alligator loafers. I loved everything about him.

"Well, look who's home. My favorite sweethearts in the whole world." Mr. Clementine hugged everyone, and said, "Sit down, my pretties, and I'll take care of everything." He always called us his "pretties," which reminded me of the wicked witch in The Wizard of Oz. But he was anything but.

Coco barked, sliding on the dark, smooth, polished wood floors like Lou Brock heading into home plate. She hopped up on Caroline's lap, jumping up and down, landing kisses on Caroline's cheeks. Mr. Clementine had a purple silk ribbon tied around Coco's neck, and had spritzed her with Chanel No. 5, which was the same perfume that Mama wore. I closed my eyes and breathed in every sweet note.

Clementine's was on Gravois Avenue, which was the most perfect street in the universe, just one street over from the most perfect address in the universe, 3 Shady Tree Drive. Caroline and I adored it, not only because Aunt Dodo and Uncle Herman lived there, but because when you entered the front door, the first thing you saw was a wedding portrait of Mama and Daddy, her long satin train swept around to the front, her bouquet of white roses and sweet gardenias held slightly to the side, and that smile—a smile of such conviction that only something unfathomable could erase it.

# CHAPTER 10

T he red, brown, and white bricks on the bungalow at 3 Shady Tree Drive were aligned in a zigzag pattern that reminded me of the teeth on a zipper. An inverted wrought iron S adorned the top of the chimney, which was separated from two gables on either side of the pitched roof. Concrete steps led to the arched, heavy wooden front door, with its small, stained-glass window. To the right of the door was a brass letter box, slender and flush with the brick façade. Caroline and I had been fascinated with it since we were toddlers. We couldn't wait 'til morning, when we would stand at the inside entry and watch the mail float like magic onto the polished wood floor. We would scamper about collecting letters in colorful envelopes, tossing aside anything that suggested ordinariness.

I was an avid stamp collector, folding them neatly and storing them in the long, slender, Velveeta Cheese wood box that I found in Aunt Dodo's attic one desperately hot July afternoon. When I was in first grade, Aunt Dodo sent three—she always sent three of every stamp she sent—stamps of a nurse wearing a little white cap and a blue and white striped uniform, lighting a candle. (I once asked her why she sent three every time, and she told me it was because that was her and Uncle Herman's favorite number—one for her, one for Uncle Herman, and one for God. "That way, everybody's covered," she would say.) I looked and looked at that stamp, and decided right then that I wanted to be a nurse when I grew up. I asked Mama for a tiny, tiny picture of me, but she couldn't find one tiny enough for me to paste over the postage stamp's nurse's face. I wanted to see what I would look like in that uniform and cap.

I became a Girl Scout Brownie in the second grade, and had my picture taken holding up three Girl Scout stamps. I wanted to paste them on my head, but Mama said, "Absolutely not, Miss Lucy."

The postman arrived at precisely 10:05 every morning. Prince Albert pipe tobacco wafted through the letter box, and each letter carried its buttery, nutty, sweet aroma. Caroline and I would hold each letter to our nostrils, close our eyes, inhale, and be reminded of Mama's nut rolls that she made every Christmas. They had the tiniest chips of walnuts and pecans, Land 'O Lakes butter, and the intoxicating aroma of pure vanilla. After Mama added the extract from the bean, she would smile, tell us to close our eyes, and slowly wave the vanilla pod back and forth, back and forth, like a church fan.

This morning, I was looking at the envelopes for more Christmas stamps of the weathervane angel with a trumpet. Christmas stamps were my favorite. Although Christmas was officially over, people always bought more Christmas stamps than they needed, so figuring that they would use those up before buying new ones, I expected to pick up a few more. I was wrong. I did find one envelope that had two from 1964, though. I already had several from that year. It was a series of four Christmas stamps: holly, mistletoe, poinsettia, and sprig of conifer. The two I found this morning were two poinsettias, which were my least favorite of the series. I decided to leave them on the envelope.

After Caroline and I sifted through the mail, we both noticed at almost the same time that Mama and Daddy's wedding portrait had been taken down from the wall; an outline of the frame and a lone nail on the wall eerily gazing back at us. We gathered up the rest of the mail and ran like the dickens through the short hallway, past the bedroom, sliding right into a seat at the kitchen table.

"My goodness gracious!" Uncle Herman exclaimed. "Are you two okay?"

"We're fine. Just a little out of breath," Caroline said. She winked at me and poked me in the side, the combination of which always meant "don't say anything."

Uncle Herman owned a printing business, and he sat at the kitchen table with a pad of paper that had Roling Printing Company at the top in black, bold, block lettering. There were columns of figures being added, subtracted, and multiplied. There were dates and the headings house payment, car payment, insurance, St. Ann's, food, clothing, gas, etc. I wondered what the etc. stood for that wasn't already mentioned in the list. He quickly folded the piece of paper and put it inside his shirt pocket, HJR monogrammed in black thread at the pocket's center. Then he winked, and I wondered at the power of such a simple gesture and three letters from the alphabet.

# CHAPTER 11

"Good morning merry sunshine,
How did you wake so soon?
You've scared the little stars away,
And shined away the moon.
I saw you go to sleep last night,
Before I ceased my playing,
How did you get way over there,
And where have you been staying?"
"I never go to sleep dear child,
I just go 'round to see
My little children of the East,
Who rise and watch for me.
I waken all the birds and bees,
And flowers on my way,
And now come back to see the child
Who stayed out late to play."

—Unknown

As long as I can remember, Aunt Dodo woke us with the sing-song of this lullaby. Her melodic voice drifted through the bedroom, like a soft breeze. I pulled the pink flower basket quilt up to my chin. I could hear the faint gliding of her house slippers on the polished wood floors and pretended to still be asleep. She never rushed through the verses, and sang with the gentleness mimicked only by bluebirds and young children. When she started the second verse, she walked over to me and brushed my bangs to the side and kissed my forehead. Her kiss was powdery, and the scent of Emeraude made me want to put the last verse into slow motion, hanging on to the word play. As she left my cheek, a wispy strand of her fine silver hair that had escaped her tortoise comb lingered.

"Are you going to sleep the day away?" Mama asked, walking into the room, lifting the shades, and squeezing my toes underneath the quilt.

"Come on, Lucy, get up," Caroline snapped. "We've got to make out the grocery list for Foley's."

I threw back the quilt, jumped off the high four-poster bed and slid across the floor to the kitchen. Caroline was already dressed in her navy corduroys, a white Peter Pan collar peeking out from her red, cable-knit Christmas sweater. She was wearing Aunt Dodo's pearl necklace, which she wore every day whenever we visited and which made me so envious I couldn't see straight. Her shoulder length, honey-colored hair shone with the sun's rays streaming through the window. I decided then and there that my final decision had been made. I wanted to be her when I grew up.

She had a brand new Roling Printing Company pad, and held Uncle Herman's fancy fountain pen in her hand like a fine violin bow.

"Okay, here's what I have so far," she said in her most annoying tone, letting me know that she was in charge. Her handwriting was as neat as the stylized letters spelling out Roling Printing Company—bold and definite. If she made a mistake, which she seldom did, she never crossed it out. Instead, she tore off the offending sheet and started over with a fresh one.

Boiled Ham

Gerber Baby Foods

Rye Bread

Apples, Oranges, and Bananas

5 Pork Chops

Applesauce

Corn

Green beans

Potatoes

Tomatoes

Lettuce

Pablum

"What else?" she said, tucking her hair behind her ears.

"Zwieback Toast," Uncle Herman said.

"Vess Red Sode," I bellowed. Aunt Dodo never said soda. She always called it sode, with a long e.

"How about some oatmeal?" Mama suggested.

We heard the clink of the milk bottles outside the kitchen door. Mr. Swensen always brought the milk up the back stairs to the screened-in porch, gently knocking to check with Aunt Dodo to see if she wanted anything special from his truck. The glass milk bottles had Bailey Farm Dairy written in flowing red cursive lettering. Caroline had a pint size bottle at home on her desk, where she kept her pens and pencils. I coveted it, and I devoted an interminable amount of time trying to devise a plan that would convince her to give me that bottle. But, so far, nothing had worked.

"Well, good morning Mr. Swensen," Uncle Herman said.

"How are you, Mr. Roling, Mrs. Roling?"

Even though Sister Theresa never even wore a slight brush of white chalk on her tunic and nary (another word I simply adore) a strand of chestnut hair escaped her habit, Mr. Swensen came in a close second in terms of cleanliness. The trousers of his white, starched uniform didn't even have any wrinkles in them, although he drove that truck around town all day long. It perplexed me as to how he was able to do that. I mean, you can't stand up and drive. And after getting in and out of that truck all day long, hauling bottles of milk and crates filled with ice cream, cottage cheese, and creamy butter, his white uniform matched Sister Theresa's white habit impeccably, and his hands were spotless, with even-cut nails, closely-trimmed cuticles, and not a hint of dirt underneath his fingernails. I stood looking up at Mr. Swensen with awe and admiration, and more than a slight bit of embarrassment, especially since I had painted my nails red for Christmas and some of the paint was beginning to chip. My hair was disheveled from last night's slumber, and a bruise was forming on my leg from a collision with my suitcase. Caroline's nail polish, on the other hand, was still as perfect as when she had finished painting them on Christmas Eve, her hair was neatly coiffed, and her collar crisp. Sister Theresa's incessant morning chant whirled in my head: "Cleanliness is next to Godliness," which only seemed to make matters worse.

"And Miss Caroline, Miss Lucy, and who else do we have with us today?"

"Mr. Swensen," Uncle Herman said with social formality, "this sweet little bundle of cotton is Miss Grace."

Grace smiled at Mr. Swensen, and he patted her on the head.

"Anything special today?"

"Well, let's see," Aunt Dodo said. "How about some chocolate milk, vanilla ice cream, and some whipped cream?"

"Be right back." Mr. Swensen took each snow-covered step carefully, his white uniform blending in, making him appear as a mirage in the desert.

"Thanks so much, Mr. Swensen," Uncle Herman said, as he handed off the slick milk bottle to Mama.

"See you next week," Mr. Swensen said, and he waved goodbye.

I watched Mr. Swensen get back inside his truck, just to make sure that he wasn't standing up, but was indeed seated, as he drove away.

"Okay, back to the list everyone," Caroline commanded.

"Anything else?"

"Oh, I almost forgot," Mama said. "Limburger cheese, please."

Caroline and I looked at each other, pinching our noses at the thought of that stinky cheese that Mama just loved.

"Got it," Caroline said as she drew a double line at the bottom of the list. Uncle Herman always drew a double line when he was finished with a mathematical calculation. I grabbed the pen from Caroline's hand, and quickly scratched a double line beneath her double line. She snatched the pen from my hand, ripped off the grocery list from the pad, and started over.

# CHAPTER 12

Mama made the absolute best pork chops in the universe. Aunt Dodo's black cast iron skillet was seasoned with oil and butter, and sizzled just a bit before Mama placed the chops on the bottom. Then, as they simmered, Mama added tiny bits of chopped onion and thinly-sliced red and green bell peppers to the skillet. The crackling sound and the aroma traveled through the dining room and into the living room, where Caroline and I were watching *The Andy Griffith Show*. Grace reached for the clown rattle that I held over her little blue eyes, and every now and then I let her win, just to see her little hand wave the rattle, the clown performing awkward somersaults.

The pork chops were succulent—a new word I picked up from Clementine's menu, beside the filet mignon entrée. I didn't much care for the succotash, but ate it anyway because I thought it might bring a smile to Mama's face. It didn't. The fried potatoes and onions were slightly crisp and the applesauce was ice cold. I had to send a stream of cool breath over the fried potatoes before sliding them into my mouth. (I always get a kick out of blowing on hot food until I can eat it.) Mama just looked at me and rolled her eyes. I laughed, and she tapped her finger on the table. Aunt Dodo giggled, and Mama tapped her finger again and said, "You, too." Then everybody laughed, including Mama. I beamed with accomplishment.

"That was simply delicious, Maggie. You could give Jake a run for his money."

Uncle Herman scooted back his green vinyl chair, making a squeaking sound on the polished yellow and white checked linoleum floor. He picked up his plate and carried it to the sink, stopping to kiss Mama lightly on the cheek as she stood washing dishes, looking out at the snow-covered lawn.

"Well, ladies, if you'll excuse me, I think I'll go see what Matt Dillon is up to, and sneak in a couple Camels while I'm at it." He opened the door to the enclosed porch and pulled it shut until it caught. We heard the springs of his rocker moan, as he settled in for another episode of *Gunsmoke*.

"Aunt Dodo, can we go upstairs to the attic?"

"Now what on earth could you two find up there that you haven't already seen a hundred times?"

"You never know," Caroline said.

"Well, my dearies, if you insist, be my guests. Let me know if you find any true fortunes up there. We can then all take a jet plane and fly to Florida."

Ever since last summer, Aunt Dodo hid the keys to the attic and basement doors after everyone went to bed. She was the only one who knew where they were. Every morning they would magically reappear, on top of the wooden shelf with black wrought iron scrolled brackets. It was secured to the wall above the television in the tiny vestibule off of the kitchen.

One night last summer, Mama went to check on us to see if we were asleep and discovered that Caroline was not in bed. Mama looked all over the house for her.

I thought Aunt Dodo's basement was the scariest place in the universe, but Caroline didn't seem to mind it. The only time I ever went down there was when Caroline dropped her dirty clothes down the laundry chute. I loved to see them billow out like fresh sheets onto the basement floor. Then I'd run like mad back up the stairs, slamming the door behind me, bending over to catch my breath.

Aunt Dodo and I followed Mama through the house as she searched for Caroline. I reminded Mama that maybe she was in the attic or in the basement with the lights on reading a book, because she had done that before.

I cowered behind Aunt Dodo, and suddenly the basement door knob turned, a creak to wake the dead. We all jumped back, including Mama. Caroline entered the hallway, closed the door, set the key back in its place on the shelf, and tucked herself back into bed. I went to hug her tight as she walked through the door, but Mama pulled me back. She put her finger to her lips, and for some unknown reason I started to cry. She smoothed my hair and hugged me to her. After Caroline was back in bed, Mama said, "You never want to wake a sleepwalker. They will be okay, and return to their bed as if nothing happened." That's when Aunt Dodo began to hide the keys. And that was the last and only time Caroline ever walked in her sleep. After all, if you don't have the key to the basement or the attic, what's the point?

40

# CHAPTER 13

The attic steps curved midway and creaked all the way to the top. In the summertime it was blazing hot, and in the winter, icy cold. We loved it no matter what the temperature. Tonight we each wore one of Uncle Herman's flannel shirts, which smelled like a combination of printer's ink, Camels, and cedar. I hugged it close to my body, inhaling the intoxicating aromas.

Caroline was scooting boxes around, opening and closing lids.

"Whatcha looking for?"

"Shhhh. Be quiet."

"Why?"

"Because."

"Because why?"

"Lucy. Stop it."

"Why?" I laughed, and Caroline shoved me to the side. A stack of Famous-Barr Department Store hat boxes tumbled to the floor.

"Oh for heaven's sake, Lucy, be still."

"Why?"

"Because I said so."

"Caroline, what are you looking for?"

"Something."

"What?"

"Mama and Daddy's wedding portrait."

"Why?"

"If you ask me why one more time, I'm gonna... Oh, here it is."

I scrambled up from underneath the pile of hat boxes, and Caroline gasped.

"What's wrong?"

"Nothing. Let's go."

Caroline stumbled to her feet, tripping on the edge of a faded white wood frame.

"You found it!"

"Lucy, let's go."

"I don't want to. I want to see Mama and Daddy's wedding picture."

"It's a portrait; a wedding portrait, not picture."

"Okay, okay. I want to see Mama and Daddy's wedding *portrait*."

"Hey, Lucy. What's that box underneath the window?"

"Don't try to change the subject, Caroline."

I walked over to Caroline, and she began to cry. Caroline never cried, and it scared me.

"Caroline? What's the matter?"

"Please Lucy, don't come over here."

"Why?"

"Because I don't want you to see Mama and Daddy's wedding picture."

I wanted to say "*portrait*," but I knew it wasn't the time to be a smart aleck. I wanted Caroline to stop crying. My eyes began to water and I tried to stop the tears from falling, but it was like trying to suck out only a portion of the nectar from the pods of the honeysuckle vine outside my bedroom window.

Caroline fell to the floor, the boards creaking as she landed, her hands covering her face. Her sobs grew stronger, and her shoulders were shaking—a shake that without the sobs could be mistaken for a laugh, like the one we shared when someone tripped on a sidewalk and turned around to look, like it was the sidewalk's fault. That always cracked us up.

I sat down beside Caroline and put my arm around her, just like she did to me when Mama scolded me for cutting my bangs by myself. (I always got them too short and uneven, like blades of grass.) I had never before in all my life put my arm around Caroline; I suddenly stopped crying and held her gently, as she buried her face against Uncle Herman's soft flannel shirt.

My foot was close enough to the edge of the frame that I could press my heel inside and scoot it towards me. Caroline's sobs masked the slight scraping noise, and I inched it out, stopping every now and then for just a second so that Caroline would not hear its approach. I wanted to see what she had seen, but at the same time not wanting to see it at all, like the summer Aunt Dodo's neighbor's son

42

Mike's little sister somehow got a piece of broken glass inside her nose, and Uncle Herman was the only one she would let try to dislodge it. We all wanted to look, but as he carefully pulled it out, we all snapped our heads away from it, closed our eyes, and scrunched up our faces. By the way, Mike, who is a year older than me is quite possibly the cutest boy in the entire world. Whenever I am around him, I can barely make a complete sentence, but he smiles at me anyway and talks up a storm.

As the frame crept farther out from where Caroline had shoved it, my daddy's face looked like it had been crushed with a hammer; the sunken spot caved in, holding onto the last remaining fiber of the heavy canvas.

Caroline raised her head and looked at me. We both sat motionless, looking at the mangled portrait. Caroline reached over and pulled our daddy's face loose from the board and put it in the pocket of Uncle Herman's brown plaid shirt that she was wearing. Then she kicked back the frame and said, "Come on, Lucy, let's go."

I stood up and began to walk down the stairs with Caroline one step behind me.

# CHAPTER 14

T he snow had lasted for several days, and L shapes of it had gathered in the corners of the windows. But it had started to rain right before supper. Cars swished by the house through puddles of water, sending another rain shower upon the already saturated lawn. Caroline sat at the kitchen table with her hand touching the pocket of her borrowed shirt, reassuring herself that Daddy's mangled face was still there.

Caroline and I had not told anyone that we had found the wedding portrait, much less divulge that Caroline had tugged at Daddy's face until she pried it from the canvas. She carried it around with her everywhere, and every now and then patted the shirt's breast pocket to make sure it had not somehow floated out of its hiding place and into oblivion.

"Caroline, honey, please sit up straight, and get your hair out of your eyes."

Caroline's hair was always perfectly in place, each strand as neat as if separated and straightened individually by a very fine-toothed comb. She always wore a tortoise headband. But tonight her auburn hair hung loose and disheveled. She reached up and tucked each side behind her ears.

"You two are acting a bit peculiar," Aunt Dodo said. Caroline and I loved the word peculiar, and Aunt Dodo was the only person we'd ever heard use it. If you looked up the definition in the dictionary, I'll bet it says something like, "Used only by Dora Ann Roling, 3 Shady Tree Drive, St. Louis, Missouri."

"Oh, we're fine," I said, trying to sound a bit too much like a grown-up.

Mama looked at me, smiled, wrinkled her forehead, and took another sip of coffee.

Caroline was looking straight ahead with a dead stare, her eyes fixed on nothing.

It gave me the creeps to watch Caroline, and yet I wanted her to be okay. To snap out of it. I wanted the goose bumps that seemed to travel up and down my arms to stop. Caroline looked like Tippi Hedren after she was attacked by the birds in the upstairs bedroom of the farm house in the movie *The Birds*. It was the scariest movie we had ever seen. And then I suddenly remembered a story that Aunt Dodo had told us one time, about a lady she knew who went crazy one day; her husband came home to find her painting the kitchen walls with mustard. Mustard! Aunt Dodo said that the woman's husband had found her on the ladder, mustard not only on the walls, but all over her, too. He told everyone that she was in a "dead stare." If it hadn't been a true story, it probably would have been very funny. I hoped that Caroline wasn't going crazy.

I scooted closer to Mama, and she said, "Lucy, what in the world is wrong with you two tonight?"

"Nothing, Mama. I'm just..."

"Oh, my God. Caroline? Caroline?"

Caroline's eyelids slowly closed, her head dipped, and she slid out of her chair onto the floor, crumpled like a rag doll.

Mama jumped up from her chair and rushed around the table, knocking over her coffee cup, coffee dripping onto the knees of my cords.

Everyone rushed over to Caroline, and Grace and I both began to cry.

"Mama, what's wrong with Caroline?"

Mama was patting Caroline's cheeks, and Uncle Herman was running water over a cloth, rushing to Caroline's side and placing it on her forehead. Aunt Dodo was holding Grace, patting her on the back, saying, "Shhhh, sweet baby, everything's okay."

Caroline slowly opened her eyes, patted the pocket of Uncle Herman's flannel shirt, tears streaking her pale face, panicked that Daddy's mangled picture was no longer there.

I spotted Daddy's picture above her soft shoulder, and scooped it up, like in a game of jacks. I felt a bit like a character in a Nancy Drew novel, realizing that no one had seen the picture of Daddy, nor me scooping it up with such aplomb, since all eyes were glued to Caroline.

"Everything's fine, Caroline," I said, and I winked and patted my shirt pocket, suddenly discovering the power of such a small gesture.

# CHAPTER 15

"I'm going to call Dr. Crookshanks," Aunt Dodo said. She scurried to the hallway and picked up the black telephone's receiver.

That telephone was scary. Caroline and I had both heard it being dialed during the middle of the night throughout our summer vacations, but no one was ever there. I swear; it was just the single, slow-moving dial of a telephone. I don't know what Caroline did when she heard it, but I always drew all the covers up over my head and prayed to Jesus that it was just my imagination.

"No, let's wait just a bit," Mama called out. "I think she's going to be fine."

Uncle Herman had picked Caroline up and carried her to the pale pink damask sofa that sat underneath the double window in the dining room.

Aunt Dodo's dining room is the most fabulous room in the entire house. No one ever eats at the dining room table, because it is piled high with magazines, newspapers, mail, and shoe boxes filled with pennies, nickels, and dimes—you can take anything from the shoe boxes to pay for candy at Foley's, ice cream at Velvet Freeze, or a burger at White Castle. No questions asked. HELP YOURSELF is written in all different crayon colors on top of each box. It is simply divine. There are drawings Caroline and I made when we were little; framed pictures of us when we were babies; a brown velvet, straw-stuffed bunny rabbit pin cushion; and a gigantic cut-glass crystal bowl filled to the brim with pencils, pens, paperclips, buttons, spools of thread, and pop bottle caps.

Every summer vacation, Caroline and I carry the heavy bowl to the kitchen and dump everything out on top of the chocolate brown speckled chrome kitchen table. Everything clinks on top of the table, marbles roll to the edge and tiny rubber balls chase after them. One time we both grabbed at a furry rabbit's foot keychain until Aunt Dodo found another one at the bottom, so we could each have one to rub for good luck.

There is a china cabinet filled to the brim with dishes, cups and saucers, bowls, Hummel figurines, a huge golden glass peacock, wedding and anniversary cake toppers, and about a million holy cards propped up against everything else. Some of them have the "Hail Mary" on the back, and lots of them have somebody's name, birth date, and date of death. Caroline and I think these are creepy, and we wipe our hands against our clothes whenever we pick one up, quickly putting it back against the teacups and bowls.

Uncle Herman's desk looks like a fish out of water. (I think that's so funny: a fish out of water.) Anyway, it is perfect! There are little compartments on the inside that neatly hold envelopes of various sizes, greeting cards, sharpened pencils, and postage stamps. There is a small framed picture of him and Aunt Dodo taken in Arizona; Uncle Herman is dressed in crisp, perfectly-pleated brown trousers and a white dress shirt. He has his sleeves rolled up, and is wearing a wide-brimmed straw hat, his hand gently placed at the bend of Aunt Dodo's arm. I love the plaid summery dress she wears, belted at the waist. I want to jump into the pocket of her dress and then pop out and grab that Indian beaded purse she has on her wrist. I think it's the most beautiful thing in the world, and I've wanted it for as long as I can remember. So does Caroline.

"Caroline, honey," Mama says, with such tenderness I want to cry. "How do you feel? Does your stomach hurt? Do you have a headache? Do you feel dizzy?"

We are all standing over Caroline, looking down at her like we are in a film being directed by Alfred Hitchcock. Aunt Dodo once told us that Hitchcock liked to give his audience a picture of the set by panning the scene from an elevated height. Every time we would sneak and watch a Hitchcock movie, Caroline and I raced to see who could find a scene in the movie that was filmed from looking down onto the set. She always found it first. But then, *I* always found "Hitch." He made an appearance in almost every film he made. My favorite was from *North by Northwest*, when he goes to board a city bus and the doors close before he can get on.

"I feel fine, Mama," Caroline says in a weak voice.

"Mama?"

"Yes, Sweetheart?"

"I need to tell you something," Caroline says, and she looks at me with tears forming in her eyes.

"Tomorrow, sweetie. For now, why don't you close your eyes and fall asleep? I'll be here by your side when you wake up, and then we can talk about it. Okay?"

"Okay."

"Sweet dreams, baby."

# CHAPTER 16

Even though I am still scared about Daddy leaving and Caroline fainting—I've never seen anyone faint before—and knowing that our visit is about to end, and wishing Mama would stop crying, and wondering if Mike will ever kiss me one day when I get older, everyone goes to bed early. Right before Caroline drifted off to sleep, she and Mama retreated to Aunt Dodo's and Uncle Herman's bedroom, Caroline tucked securely underneath Mama's arm, the crisp white quilt pulled up to their chins. Aunt Dodo and Uncle Herman slept in the guest room, with sweet little Grace beside them in the crib they'd bought for our visit. They never missed anything. I cowered underneath Uncle Herman's crazy quilt. His mother made it for him when he was born; Aunt Dodo always kept it draped over the back of that luscious pink damask sofa that sits underneath the dining room window, facing Nick's Tavern across the street. I fingered each piece of the quilt, finding soft velvets, rich silks, and fine embroidery. Aunt Dodo kissed me goodnight, and I felt her tears lightly touch my cheeks. I thought she was thinking about the same things I was, except for wondering whether Mike would ever kiss her.

Once the lights had been turned off, the red and green neon lights of the small Christmas tree in Nick's window flashed off and on, summoning me to my knees to look at the falling snowflakes. I wanted to go outside, to make snowmen and angels. I caught a tear with my tongue and tried to imagine it was a snowflake. I rested my hands on my chin, and Daddy waved at me. At first I thought I was dreaming. I closed my eyes and shook my head, like I'd seen on television. When I opened my eyes, he blew me a kiss. I scurried back under the indigo quilt, rubbing the rabbit's foot that I'd brought to bed with me; I was too scared to call out for anyone, even God himself.

# CHAPTER 17

n the morning, I am the first one to check to see if the mail has arrived. There, on the polished wood floor, is a single piece of mail. Written on the front of the white envelope is my name, and Caroline's, and Grace's. The handwriting is Daddy's—strong, bold strokes with a heart crowning the top of the *i* in Caroline's name. I start shaking so bad that at first I can't pick up the envelope. It is sealed, and I wonder if I should wait until I am with Caroline to read it. But she is still sleeping, and I am too impatient to wait—I am also too scared to open it. I start to open the envelope, then stop. Start and then stop again, like the first time I rode the roller coaster at the fair. One minute I was ready to hand the man my ticket, and the next minute I changed my mind. But once I rode it, I couldn't get enough of it. I wanted to ride it and ride it over and over until the fair left town, and I was anxious for its arrival the next summer. Finally, I decide to slide my fingers under the sealed flap and read.

*Dear Caroline, Lucy, and sweet little Grace. I knew that your mama would bring you for a visit to Aunt Dodo's and Uncle Herman's. That is why I came, too. I know you are having fun. You always loved to come here. Even though no one knows I am here, I wanted to be able to see you, even if it was from a distance. I called last night, but hung up when Uncle Herman answered the phone. I knew that I would not be welcomed—ever again. I hope I did not frighten you last night Lucy, when you saw me wave from Nick's. You just looked so sweet, and I feel like I haven't seen you in a long time, even though it hasn't yet been a week. Walking away from each of you on that windy Christmas day was the hardest thing I have ever done, but I had* a higher purpose than being your father—or thought I did. I miss each of you so much already, but I had to do what I did. Know that I will always love you, and that what I did I thought was best for each of you, was best for every child. And yet, there is some uncertainty that is beginning to lurk. I know now that what I did could have been wrong. No, it was wrong, but at the time I thought it was right. I know I sound crazy. Maybe I am. I am so sorry and so confused. I keep seeing their eyes. Not just those two boys, but every boy's eyes that we ever hurt. There are nights I wake up in a cold sweat and shudder, and all I see are pairs of eyes circling in my head. They are all the same, and yet all different. They torture me, and they will blind me in the end. It is just a matter of time. I also know that I will never see any of you again. I have hurt your mama so deeply. I don't think she will ever forgive me. I am in a lot of trouble, and even now I can't believe that I did what I did to all those young colored boys. And not just me, but my friends too. In my mind, they are now colored boys, not niggers. But the damage has been done. I didn't pull the trigger, as they say, but I didn't stop Scooter and the others from doing it. God in Heaven forgive me. With every word I write, I am ashamed. It strikes me like a bullet penetrating my heart, and I can't breathe. The more I write the more I am certain that I was wrong. I will not say any more—and perhaps have said too much already—because I don't want you to have to lie if you are asked if you knew anything about what I did. I will not contact you anymore, and I am going to be on the run until I am caught because, as you know, you always get caught. It is just a matter of time. You three girls and your mama are the best things that ever happened to a broken down man like me. When you hear about everything I did, please find it in your hearts to forgive me. I know it won't be easy, and I probably don't deserve it, but my prayer will be that you will forgive me and love me with all my faults. Love, Daddy.

"Holy Shit! What the hell is going on?" Even I can't believe these words were whispered from my lips as I slide to the corner, fold the paper, and place it back inside the envelope. I sit crouched in the corner, hugging my knees to my chest, crying harder than I ever thought possible. My shoulders won't stop shaking, like they have a mind of their own, like they feel every letter of every word that was written. Once again, I shift from wanting to rush to Mama and show her the letter, rush to Caroline and let her tell me what to do with it, or keep it to myself. Until I can decide what to do, I will keep it to myself, folding it in half and tucking it safely in the back pocket of my Levi's.

I want desperately to tell Caroline about last night and about the letter from Daddy, but she still isn't acting like herself. When I manage to stand up and put one foot in front of the other, I walk into the kitchen. She is in a dead stare one minute and perfectly alert the next; I want so much to go to her and squeeze her so tight so that I can make everything hurting inside her go away. Everything painful inside me, too. But it is too late for that now; nothing will ever be the same. If I tell Mama about the letter, she could either get really upset and start to cry or take it from me and tear it up into a million little pieces. Neither option seems like a good one. Besides, there has already been enough crying to fill up Aunt Dodo's claw-footed bathtub, so I decide to stick to my plan of keeping it all a secret—seeing Daddy wave at me from Nick's and reading the letter he left for us this morning. I keep trying to put together all the pieces of the puzzle. Little by little, it is all starting to come together, even though I am not sure I want it to. Sometimes, like Father Tim says, it is best to weigh all options and then choose. *Time is on my side. I think.* Suddenly, I think about confession. Wouldn't Daddy be forgiven if he went to confession? Then I remember something called repentance and the tears begin again, but this time they stay locked inside, refusing to show themselves to anyone. Then I think of Grace, and wish with all my heart that I was just a baby.

Mama is brushing Caroline's hair, pulling it back into a pony tail, and tying a navy and dark green plaid ribbon into a bow at the back. Caroline looks at me, winks, and smiles. That rabbit's foot is finally working. I run to her and put both arms around her neck, and she does the same to me. She whispers in my ear, "Lucy, do you have it?"

"Got it," I say.

"Why don't you two go watch TV?" Mama says. "I think it's about time for *Bewitched.*" *Oh, to be Samantha.. That way, we could fix everything with a wiggle of our noses.*

# CHAPTER 18

"It couldn't have been," Caroline said, when I told her I saw Daddy the night before, at Nick's window. Even though I managed to keep part of my secret for a while, I had to tell somebody. I thought it best to tell Caroline. She would know whether or not to tell Mama.

"But I saw him. It really was Daddy."

"It could have been just a nice man who was waving to a little girl."

"But he blew me a kiss, Caroline. If he was just any ole man, he wouldn't have blown me a kiss, would he?"

"I don't know, Lucy, maybe not. But what would Daddy be doing at Nick's?"

"Maybe he was watching us when we left, and figured we would be coming here to see Aunt Dodo and Uncle Herman." Now I was faced with knowing that I had to share Daddy's letter with her so that she would know I hadn't just *thought* I'd seen Daddy, but that I really had seen him last night at Nick's.

"But then, why didn't he just come over and knock on the door to see us? Why would he just sit there and stare out the window?"

"I don't know." But the truth was, I did know. I just didn't know if I was ready to show her the letter. At the time it was something that only I knew about, and I was still worried that Caroline wasn't strong enough to handle it. But then again, Caroline was strong enough to handle anything. "I keep thinking about Mama and Daddy's wedding portrait. I can't believe that Aunt Dodo or Uncle Herman would have destroyed it. Can you? I mean, it was smashed to smithereens. And not just anywhere, either. It's like the head of the hammer was aimed directly and intentionally at Daddy's face. It had to have been one of them. Nobody else lives here."

"I don't know. I'm sure there's a reason, although I can't imagine what he could have done that would have made them do that. It had to have been really bad, though. Why didn't they just throw the portrait away, instead of smashing in Daddy's face? Maybe Mama doesn't want to be with him anymore. Remember when Elizabeth's mother and father got a divorce last year? When I asked Mama about it, she said that sometimes marriages don't work out, and people get a divorce. She said that Elizabeth's father fell in love with someone else."

"How do you fall in love with someone else? Do you think Mama and Daddy still love each other? How do you stop loving somebody, even if they do something really terrible? Caroline, I'm scared."

"I'm scared too. Hey, Lucy?"

"What?"

"Remember when we were in Mama and Daddy's room looking for our Christmas presents? They were downstairs, and we were trying to find out where they hid the presents. Anyway, we tried to open Daddy's closet, but it was locked. I remember thinking it was weird that his closet was locked. I mean, I don't remember any doors in our house ever being locked. And then I forgot about it, until now. I wonder why it was locked?"

"You're right. It *was* locked. That's when we found lots of presents underneath the bed. By the way, that's sort of a silly place to hide Christmas presents. Why do you think Daddy's closet was locked?"

"I don't know, but as soon as we get home, that's the first place I'm going to go."

"Me, too." And yet, in my heart, I knew that we would never go back to Germantown.

"Hey, Lucy?"

"What?"

"Where's Daddy's picture?"

"I hid it in my Velveeta box, underneath everything else."

"Where's the box?"

"It's inside the TV cabinet, behind the TV."

"Good place."

"Yeah."

"Go get it."

"Okay. I'll be right back."

Even though I was scared to death about everything that was happening, I was so happy that Caroline and I were playing sleuths, just like Nancy Drew. That's who we needed: Nancy Drew.

When I reached the living room, I opened the doors of the TV cabinet, reached behind it, and pulled out the Velveeta Cheese box. I hid it under my sweater, and the roughness of the wooden box left a splinter in my stomach. "Ouch," I cried, trying to muffle the sound of my own voice. When I looked down, there was a drop of blood the size of a pinpoint, but it was enough to make me pick up my speed, anxious to get back to Caroline.

"Come on," she said. "Let's go down to the basement. No one will see us there."

"But I hate the basement, Caroline."

"Oh, for heaven's sake, Lucy. I hate it too, but there's nobody down there."

"Why can't we just stay upstairs?"

"Because we can't."

"Why?"

"Because we might get caught, and someone might see the picture."

"Well, okay, let's go then."

Aunt Dodo's basement was the scariest place on earth. There were more dark corners than in any scary movie, and the wire coat hangers that hung on a line by the washer and dryer were always moving back and forth. The cinder block walls were a putrid brown, like the color of vomit on a schoolroom floor. Mama hated the word vomit, and made us say "throw-up" instead. Throw-up didn't have near the same impact, but Mama was a stickler for proper social etiquette, so whenever we were around her we said throw-up—then we said vomit under our breaths.

The door that led to the outside steps had a crack in the glass, and slight streams of cold air crept through and brought shivers to my spine whenever I passed by. There were hanging, quilted clothes bags that housed old dresses, suits, and coats. Moth balls were scattered along the inside of the bottom of the bags. I love the smell of moth balls, and would always stop briefly, close my eyes, inhale, and smile. Underneath the creaking stairs were boxes filled with Mama's baby clothes, toys, and books. In the back corner, there was a rocking chair with a splintered cane seat. One time when we were in the cellar watching the laundry float down from the upstairs chute, we both heard the chair creak. We looked at each other, then at the chair that was rocking back and forth. We ran like Tom Robinson after he was found guilty of raping Mayella Violet Ewell.

"Lucy!"

"What?! You scared me to death, Caroline. Stop it!"

"Come over here."

"Why? Why can't we just sit here on the last step?"

"Because someone might open the door and see us, and ask us what we're doing. It will be safer over here."

I walked behind Caroline, and she stopped suddenly.

I ran right into her back, nearly knocking her over.

"For goodness sake, Lucy! Watch where you're going."

We sat down on two beach chairs, the Velveeta box sitting on my lap.

"Where did you get all this stuff, Lucy?"

"Oh, some things I found on the street corner here at Aunt Dodo's, some things I found on my way to Foley's, or Famous, or White Castle. Remember when we would walk to the library, and sometimes I would go into Goodwill? You would never go in with me, but you would wait outside until I was finished. One time, I found this little brass key, tied with a black silk ribbon."

I took out everything and laid it all on my lap. I made an "oink, oink" sound when I removed the pink-painted lead toy pig from the box, so small that it fit in the palm of my hand.

"This doll head, I found across the street on Nick's corner one day. I know she looks a bit scary, but I always wondered how her head got off her body. I mean, who would do that? So now somewhere, in this vast universe, her body is floating around—or maybe it was washed down the sewer. Ick! I mean, can you imagine, walking around without your head?"

"I love this tiny compass. It doesn't work anymore, but I like the feel of it in my palm. Here, try it. Close your eyes and rub it like a genie's lamp."

To my surprise, Caroline took the compass and rubbed it. "Please bring Daddy back."

We both laughed so hard that the Velveeta box fell from my lap, everything scattering like a game of marbles. We loved to use lines from movies, and we always thought the beginning of It's A Wonderful Life was funny, with everybody praying for George's return. Mama thought Jimmy Stewart was handsome, but Caroline and I couldn't see it. Daddy was much more handsome than Jimmy Stewart. He was just as tall and lanky, but his rich dark hair and his high cheekbones (which I got, but Caroline didn't) made him a shoe-in for the most handsome man in the world.

My laughter almost turned into tears as I gathered up the broken Mickey Mouse watch, Cracker Jack prizes, and one of Mama's brooches. Daddy's picture was turned over. I picked it up and handed it to Caroline.

Caroline tried to smooth over the rough fragments of the canvas, then kissed what remained of Daddy's image and pressed the small rectangle to her heart. "Oh, Daddy," she said. "What did you do? Where are you?"

As I scrambled to pick up the remaining pieces of my oddities, I noticed a tiny red velvet clutch. Barbie's clutch! But how did it get there?

"Hey Caroline, look."

"What?"

"Barbie's red velvet clutch. I've been looking all over for that. Remember, I told you that I lost it when I was spending the night with Diane, and I always thought she took it, because she had lost hers, but Mama told me I had no real proof, so I couldn't say anything. She laughed when I told her that the next time I was at Diane's, I was going to look closely at that red velvet clutch of hers, because mine had a tiny hole at the bottom left corner where the seam was starting to come apart. Mama wanted to know what I would do if I found it and the tiny hole was there. I told her that I hadn't worked through that yet. How in the world did it get in my box? Maybe it was there all along. How funny. Boy, am I glad that I never said anything to Diane. Holy cow!"

As I heard myself repeat this story to Caroline, I suddenly knew that I would probably never play with my Barbie dolls ever again. Something had happened to me in the past couple of weeks, and suddenly Barbie and all her dreams and myriad occupations made the ridiculousness of the lost red velvet clutch story seem like something that happened a long time ago. It made me realize that it was so inconsequential, compared to what had taken place since Christmas morning, which seemed like many years ago. And I felt different. Almost uncomfortable, like realizing that the length of your favorite jeans now hits at your ankles, or that the long sleeves of your favorite sweater have suddenly become three-quarter length. And then Caroline said, "Oh, Lucy, don't ever change. I like you just the way you are." I realized that she had been thinking the same thing, right along with me.

The door to the cellar opened, and we quickly scooped up everything and put it back in the box.

"Caroline? Lucy? Are you two down there?"

"Yes, Mama."

"What on earth are you doing in the cellar?"

Mama's footsteps descended the stairs, and Caroline and I hid the box underneath the chair.

Mama stood at the bottom of the stairs, and said, "Well? What are you doing down here?"

"Oh, nothing," Caroline said.

"We were just, uh, we were just going to find one of Aunt Dodo's fancy dresses and wear it tonight for New Year's," I said with much exhilaration, mainly because I never thought of anything to say whenever I was caught doing something I shouldn't be doing, and I was rather pleased with my response. Caroline was always the mastermind; I envied her quick nature, but now it was my time to throw my shoulders back with pride.

"Well, won't *that* be fun. Which ones are you going to wear?"

"Oh, we don't know yet," Caroline said.

"Well then," Mama said, "I'll leave you two alone so you can decide your wardrobe for the big fanfare. By the way, have you picked out the bell for the occasion?"

"Not yet," Caroline said.

A few years ago, we were here at New Year's, and Aunt Dodo came to the basement to get one of her bells. She had collected bells for as long as I could remember, and they are all displayed inside a glass cabinet. There are bells from her trips to Arizona, with the state seal on them; a brass school bell; sleigh bells on leather straps; a brass bell in the shape of a lady; a crystal bell, which we used one time when we saw one in a movie, sitting on the dinner table (the lady would ring it whenever she wanted the cook to bring her something); a miniature silver bell with a bird on top; and an old black mammy bell. The black mammy wears a red dress with white polka dots and a linen apron that hides the base of the bell. She looks just like Mammy in *Gone with the Wind*, with her shiny black face and big red lips. Our favorite, a huge brass bell that you don't ring, but instead stomp on to make a loud gong, was the one we chose to ring in the new year—the first one without Daddy.

"Well, after you select this year's bell," Mama said, "head on back upstairs."

"Yes, ma'am," we chimed. Just as Caroline was heading over to the bell collection, I pulled her back down and said, "Caroline, I have something to show you." I pulled the letter out from my back pocket. She recognized Daddy's handwriting, and a single tear rolled down her cheek as she began to read.

# CHAPTER 19

"Five, four, three, two, one! Happy New Year!"

Grace was shaking her rattle, Caroline was stomping on the bell, and Mama and Aunt Dodo were wearing pointed hats and shaking noisemakers. Mama's had a man in a tuxedo, busting a red balloon painted on it, and Aunt Dodo's had a bunch of bells painted all different colors that Uncle Herman bought at the ten-cent store. Caroline had on a black silk lace dress, and wore a black feather in her hair. I wore a gold sequined dress with a fur collar that was detachable. We both wore black high heels that we could hardly walk in, so we just stood on the front steps, along with everyone else in the neighborhood. Mike's family was setting off firecrackers, and Uncle Herman stood like Abraham Lincoln, wearing a black top hat. The orange glow from his cigarette looked like a campfire about to go out. For the first time in several days, we were all smiling and laughing.

I looked over at Nick's, and people were gathered out front on the corner, some of them tripping and falling, others trying to pick them up. I searched the crowd for Daddy, but didn't see him anywhere. I wished it *had* been just a nice old man waving to a sweet little girl; I wished it had been a dream or a story that I had made up in my mind. Maybe I would wake up in the morning and Daddy would be sitting at the kitchen table, with Grace on his lap and Mama bringing him French toast with maple syrup, bacon, and a little orange slice and a strawberry. And maybe he would blow her a kiss, and she would wink. But I knew none of that was going to happen—ever again, just like Daddy said.

# CHAPTER 20

The snow was falling softly outside the warmth of Aunt Dodo's bungalow, and I was entranced not only by that glorious frozen crystal, but also because Mama was brushing my hair with Aunt Dodo's ivory-handled brush. I had just finished taking a luxurious bath, filled to the brim with soap bubbles and the intoxicating scent of Neutrogena soap, its shiny cake slippery in my hands. I had spritzed my squeaky clean body with Emeraude, and tried to figure out how in the world I could take the smell of that fragrance, along with all the other delicious scents of 3 Shady Tree Drive, home with me to Memphis.

One year for Christmas, Aunt Dodo gave Caroline and me a Hummel figurine each. Caroline's was called On the Phone, and it was a figurine of a boy talking on the telephone. Caroline liked to make up conversations that the boy might be having. They were usually one-liners. One time she suggested, "Hey, man, what the heck do you want?" We all laughed so hard that my side hurt. One time she said, "Oh, yes, I'd love to go to the dance with you," and she curtsied.

My figurine was called Wash Day, and the little girl was hanging clothes on a line from a basket. In the springtime, Aunt Dodo liked to hang her sheets outside on the clothesline. She said nothing was as indulgent as sleeping on sheets that had been air-dried, filled with the soft breezes and scents from her rose garden. She was right, too.

Each of these figurines was wrapped securely inside one of Uncle Herman's socks and placed inside an empty Quaker Oatmeal box. That box was almost more precious to us than the figurine. We kept the boxes on a shelf in our closet, and every time we started to miss Aunt Dodo and Uncle Herman, we would retrieve those oatmeal boxes from the top shelf and gently open the lid, just enough to get our noses inside; we'd close our eyes and breathe in 3 Shady Tree Drive, placing the lid quickly back on top of the box to make sure the fragrance didn't evaporate.

I noticed that our suitcases were packed and ready by the front door. Aunt Dodo was sniffling. She always cried when we were about to leave, and Uncle Herman was holding Grace with one arm and bringing in Caroline a little closer with the other. I clung to Mama, and she said, "Now, now, you know we can't stay forever." But I didn't know. Now that Daddy was gone, why couldn't we stay forever?

At the center of the kitchen table sat the crusted photograph of our father from the wedding portrait. Even in its smallness, it seemed exaggerated. We all sat down at the table, and Mama said, "Lucy, Caroline told us this morning that you two found the wedding portrait in the attic. I thought it had been thrown away, but Aunt Dodo and Uncle Herman thought one of you might want to have it one day, so they stored it in the attic. They thought they had hidden it so that you wouldn't see what had happened to it, but like the two little detectives you are, you stumbled across it. When Uncle Herman took it down from the wall in the foyer, he had planned to hang a picture in its place. The one he had chosen was not big enough to cover the space, and you know how particular Aunt Dodo is, so they decided to leave it bare until they could buy something to put in its place." Mama was talking with such speed that I could hardly understand her, the script seemingly prepared well in advance; yet at the same time, it seemed like she was making it all up as she went along. Every now and then, she would turn her gaze towards Aunt Dodo and Uncle Herman, and they would nod in what seemed like clandestine agreement.

"When he went to take down the nail that held our wedding portrait on the wall, the hammer slipped from his hand and fell, head down, onto daddy's face, which is why it was caved in like it was. They had planned to have it restored if one of you wanted it one day, but in the meantime, they just stored it in the attic." I think if Mama had told the story without rushing to finish it, we might have believed her.

"We are so sorry that you had to find it that way, Sweetie," Uncle Herman said.

Caroline and I looked at each other, knowing that we were thinking the exact same thing. For the first time in our lives, we not only questioned Mama, we questioned Aunt Dodo and Uncle Herman, too. But it was something we kept to ourselves. Besides, from the looks on their faces, they knew what we were thinking.

"We'll just keep this part of the portrait, and see if we can find someone who knows how to repair the damage," Uncle Herman said, and he looked to Mama for affirmation. But she was in one of Caroline's deep stares, studying the image of Daddy with the same disdainful look that Scout Finch gave to Calpurnia when she told her to stop fidgeting with her dress on the first day of school.

And then, in one fell swoop, before Uncle Herman could pick it up, Caroline reached across the table and scooped up the tattered canvas. She said, "I just want to look at it one more time."

Uncle Herman looked surprised, Mama's look suddenly changed from reverie into one of fear, and Aunt Dodo's hand covered her mouth. For adults, they weren't very good at covering up their suspected guilt.

"Caroline, I forgot to get something from the bedroom," I said. I hadn't, but thought it best to leave the kitchen, at least until everyone could figure out what the next move was going to be—me included. I grabbed Caroline's hand and we went scurrying through the dining room, past the living room, and landed on the wooden floor in the foyer. We just sat and looked at each other, knowing that something other than Daddy leaving had changed. At the same time, we knew that parts of the story would probably always remain a mystery. Caroline took off her silver chain with the little cross charm on it that she got from Mama and Daddy on her First Communion, which she always wore, and slid the cross from the chain, dropping it into the pocket of her jeans. Then she slid the silver chain through a hole in the damaged canvas and closed the clasp.

She hopped up on top of the mahogany chest underneath the nail that had held the wedding portrait, and placed the chain on the nail. Daddy's face moved slightly from side to side, like a clock's pendulum. When she hopped back down off of the chest, we both stood there, looking up with a reverence that was normally reserved for the crucifix. Even after reading Daddy's letter, we still loved him. I supposed we always would. And I suddenly liked who I was, for the first time in my life—who I wanted to be when I grew up. Not any one of Barbie's adventures, not a nurse in a white cap and uniform, not Mama, and not Caroline. Just me. And in spite of, or because of, this moment that seemed to freeze in time, I was no longer as sad as I had been since Christmas day. I knew that something— everything—had changed.

Caroline made the sign of the cross and prayed, "Eternal rest grant unto him, Oh Lord, and may perpetual light shine upon him. May his soul and the souls of all the faithful departed through the mercy of God rest in peace. Amen."

"Amen."

"Lucy, I didn't show anyone the letter from Daddy. After all, it only had our names on it, not Mama's, and not Aunt Dodo's or Uncle Herman's. It is our letter. We'll keep it safe. Maybe one day Grace will want to read it and we'll show it to her, but never to anyone else." She hugged me and whispered, "I love you, Lucy." And then we walked away, Daddy's eyes swaying slightly from side to side.

# CHAPTER 21

We never did go back to Germantown, but Mama did. And we didn't find out what was locked inside Daddy's closet until right before the new school year started.

Although we pretty much knew what Daddy had done, Mama didn't know that we knew. She didn't know about the contents of the letter, and never would. But every time we asked her what happened to Daddy, she always said, "We'll talk about it some other time." Then she'd change the subject, tell us it was time for bed, or take us out for barbecue at Willie Joe's BBQ across the street from our new house on Stage Road—only it wasn't anywhere close to being "new."

When we got back to Memphis, Mama's friend Mary met us at the station and hugged Mama so tight that I didn't think she'd ever let go. I tugged at Mama's coattail like a little child, until she loosed Mary's grip and brought me to her side. Caroline was holding Grace, who was sleeping against her shoulder, and said, "Yes ma'am," when Mary asked her if she had had a good time in St. Louis. I thought it was a silly question. I mean, *of course* we had a great time in St. Louis. We always had a great time in St. Louis. Didn't Mary know that? Even though it had changed, it would always be remembered as a good time. In thinking about it, we would never allow ourselves to think of St. Louis as anything but a good time, regardless of what had happened while we were there.

"Joe's out in the car. Let's gather your bags, and we'll head out to your new place."

Caroline and I looked at each other, and Mama said, "It's okay. It's going to be okay. It's just going to be temporary, until we can find something else."

Like a bolt of lightning, the words temporary and something else sent up a red flag in my mind. It was as if Mama was trying to convince herself that whatever *it* was, it would be okay, but I had a feeling that I wasn't going to like whatever *it* was. A sense of foreboding overtook my psyche.

"But why aren't we going home?" Caroline asked. "I want to go home, Mama. To our house."

"Please, Sweetie."

"Me, too," I chimed in.

"Girls, please," Mama pleaded.

Grace squirmed, and made a kitten-like plea of her own. Caroline said, "Come on, Lucy," and gently nudged me into the unknown.

# CHAPTER 22

4321 Stage Road was tucked in between two seemingly giant precipices: on the one side, a dilapidated, yet somehow stately, crumbling stucco edifice that looked at one glance to be a large residence and at another, a defeated fortress, like the abandoned house in *The Mystery of the Ivory Charm*. The structure looked like it was once painted a deep salmon, but the color had faded to resemble that of a rotten peach. The boxwood hedge surrounding the property was overgrown with brambles, and in desperate need of a manicure. The trunk of the ailing magnolia tree didn't stand regally like the one in our yard in Germantown, but instead seemed to weep, as if bent from a long, tortuous illness. The upstairs and downstairs windows were covered with a thin coat of varnish and heavy, drawn shades that someone had trimmed without the aid of a ruling device. Each bottom edge was ragged, primitively cut. Cats of various pedigrees roamed the grounds and wove in and out of the boxwood, like bubbling blueberries seeping through Mama's baked lattice pastry pies. It was both eerie and inviting, like a scary movie scene that you know you shouldn't look at, but you do anyway, wishing later that you hadn't.

Fred's Service Station anchored the other side of our "new" house. The asphalt was cracked, and reminded me of pictures from my geography book that showed the dry, parched desert of Arizona. I was reminded instantly to use my Coty body lotion every day, so that my skin would not be scaly as I aged. There were spots of grease and oil splotched throughout the asphalt, like ink blots from my daddy's fountain pens, and empty oil cans strewn about, without rhyme or reason. They were scattered here and there, despite the overabundance of large, heavy, half-full, rusty drum trashcans. Cars in need of repair were hoisted on hydraulic lifts, old tires were stacked around the inside perimeter of the smelly garage, and trash cans beside the gas pumps were burdened with refuse from every customer, eager to unload their trash for someone else to dispose. The windows of the office were strewn with insects, and the inside window sill was home to myriad travel pamphlets, half empty soda bottles, and soiled rags. The only item of dignity was a Coca-Cola pop machine, its glistening bottles dripping with ice-cold condensation.

4321. My first thought when I let my eyes gaze up the steep hill to look at our house was that when we began to teach Grace all the important numbers to know as she got older, 4321 would be easy for her to learn. As she learned her numbers for school—1, 2, 3, 4—she could easily remember her house number was just the opposite: 4, 3, 2, 1. Simple. It was the first good thing about our new address. Maybe we'd get lucky and our new phone number would be easy for her to remember, too.

Sweet little Grace. I couldn't even begin to imagine what life was going to be like, living here at 4321 Stage Road in Raleigh, Tennessee, and it nearly killed me to think that sweet little Grace would never know Germantown. I was determined to make sure that the first thing I did when I got inside the new house was to grab my journal that Aunt Dodo and Uncle Herman got me for Christmas, and write down as much as I could remember about Germantown. I planned on drawing pictures of everything in our house and all its trimmings as well as writing down every experience we ever had as a family, so that Grace would know it, too.

The house looked like a paper cut-out, only it wasn't neatly drawn or multi-colored, and the scissors that were used to cut it from its book were not sharpened, like the scissors the teachers let you use in first grade. The steep hill that ran from the gulley at the edge of the two-lane road topped out at the center of the delicate wood structure that resembled a child's first drawing of a house: a square formation with a triangular-shaped roof. Without knowing it, I suddenly found myself holding my breath, for fear that if I exhaled, I'd huff and I'd puff and I'd blow our house down.

Matching the unkempt landscaping of our neighbor's house, the hedges surrounding our own property were in desperate need of a trim, as well. The few rose bushes in the front yard were crusted from neglect, and the trim around the windows needed to be scraped and given a shiny new coat of varnish. As we walked around to the side of the house, Mama exclaimed with the excitement of the past early Christmas morning, "Oh, my! What's that running alongside the fence? Why, I do believe it's a honeysuckle vine. Just like the one at our old house. How delightful! I can't wait for spring!" For the first time since our arrival, we all smiled at the anticipation of something as sweet as the nectar from the honeysuckle vine.

Three lopsided steps led from the base of the house to its screened front porch door. The only ornamentation on the house was a shiny brass pineapple door knocker just beyond the screened door. It seemed as out of place as we were—a pumpkin without a patch, a doll without a house or, as Father Tim would say, "a sheep without a shepherd." And yet it seemed to welcome us at the same time, reminding us of the possibilities that lay among the ruins, of the silver linings behind every cloud.

"Do you like it?" Mary asked.

I had forgotten that the Weatherlys were still there, and the sudden sound of Mary's voice startled me. Mama, too, apparently.

"Maggie? Maggie?!" Mrs. Weatherly implored.

"Oh, I'm sorry, Mary. What did you say?"

"The door knocker. Do you like it? Joe and I picked it out together."

"Oh my...well, yes, of course I do, Mary. Thank you so much for thinking of us."

And just as suddenly, much to the Weatherlys' surprise, we all burst out laughing, including the sweet giggle from Grace's tender lips. And Mama hugged Mary, who, too, laughed.

When we unlocked the front door and walked inside the house, Mama scanned the front room in a similar yet completely different way from her scan on Christmas Day, when we left Germantown. Caroline and I fought back tears, and later we both agreed that Mama had fought them back, too. There was no baby grand piano, no plush white carpeting, and no stone-stacked chimney. As a matter of fact, it was icy cold and as devoid of any ornamentation as a Christmas tree before the decorations.

# CHAPTER 23

Over the next several months, Mama worked on making 4321 Stage Road into a home for us. She said that the furniture came with the house when she agreed to rent it from her new boss, who owned lots of rental property throughout the Memphis area.

The couch in the living room was not like Aunt Dodo's pink silk damask sofa; instead, it was covered in a very scratchy, nubby fabric in dark brown, olive green, and the color of a rusted bottle cap. It was okay whenever we wore our navy corduroy school pants; but when the weather warmed up, we wouldn't even think of sitting on it, especially not when we wore our summer shorts. The springs were shot, and the fabric was beginning to thin on the seat cushions. Mama tossed some multi-colored solid throw pillows from end-to-end, which drew attention away from the couch's many flaws. The first thing Mama noticed when we walked into the house that first day was the lamps' shades on the mismatched end tables—they still had the cellophane wrapped around them. It had yellowed over time; Mama marched right up to each one, unscrewed the finial, and feverishly unwrapped the cellophane covering, balling it up like a baseball and tossing it into the plastic waste paper basket by the front door. There was a television set and a tattered rag rug on the wood floor. Mama was smiling so sweetly at us that we quickly gathered up the courage to keep hidden our incredulousness. We felt like fish out of water.

The tiny kitchen was located at the back of the house, with a screen door leading to the barren back yard. Like the gleaming brass door knocker, the glass bowl filled with fresh fruit seemed as out of place on the chipped kitchen counter, but its sweet offering of apples, bananas, grapes, and oranges, with a single lime crowning the peak brought a smile to our faces. We looked at Mama for reassurance, and she smiled and nodded. The newly-laid, shiny yellow linoleum floor was a welcomed improvement. Mama walked over to retrieve the note that was stuck in between an apple and an orange. She said, "Oh, how thoughtful. How in the world did they get that ordered so quickly?"

"Who's it from, Mama?" Caroline asked.

"Now I'll bet you can guess that one yourself."

Caroline smiled and said, "Aunt Dodo and Uncle Herman?"

"Precisely."

The bedroom that Caroline and I were going to share was located at the back of the house too, across from the kitchen. It had twin beds, one covered in a faded floral bedspread and the other draped with a green and purple striped coverlet. There was a thin, white, chenille bedspread folded and draped at the foot of each bed. The pancakes we ate for breakfast were fluffier than the pillows on the beds. Mama put her arms around us and said that first thing in the morning we could go to Penney's and get some new ones. We both smiled.

"Yeah, and maybe new sheets, too," Caroline whispered in my ear.

The one bathroom and Mama's room, where Grace would sleep, were at the front of the house. Mama's bed had a brass headboard that needed polishing, and Grace's crib was white with tiny flowers painted on its rails. The single windows in both bedrooms were the best part of each room, since they were framed by the soon-to-be blossoming honeysuckle vine.

When we went to bed that night, we all snuggled together on Mama's bed, Aunt Dodo's flower basket quilt spread over us like a smooth layer of peanut butter and strawberry preserves over freshly-baked white bread. Through the soft sniffling we slept, as Mama glanced through page after page of a stack of decorating magazines that she'd retrieved earlier from her suitcase, although I couldn't imagine why she had brought them with her. But then again, 'why' could be asked about most everything in our lives at that moment. We fell asleep, dreaming of the answers, wanting to sleep forever, and hoping that when we woke up we would say a prayer of thanksgiving that it had all been just a dream.

LUCY
SUMMER, 1966

# CHAPTER 24

"Nigger, nigger, never die
Black face, shiny eyes.
Crooked nose and teapot
Toes, and that's the way
A nigger grows."

—Unknown

The rusted screen door slammed shut as I ran down the boarded steps and landed on the parched earth, scared to death that she'd catch me and hind me good on the backside with the switch she kept propped against the door facing, for just such times. I kept running until I slid on my butt at the bottom of the hill, just short of the heavy traffic on Stage Road.

Lila was a bosomy, ebony-skinned woman who could iron a shirt until it almost stood on its own on top of the ironing board, ready any minute to bellow commands to a battalion of enlisted men; fry the juiciest apple pies in the universe; clean a bathtub—even our cracked porcelain tub—'til you could make out your silhouette; and who, when the Armeano twins threw rocks at our German Shepherd Tina, could envelope you in the ample folds of her body with such tenderness that you wanted to meld into her sphere. When I first met her, I resisted the urge to do this.

Even though she had been with us for six months, I had only recently opened myself up to this tenderness and still couldn't decide whether or not to like her, much less consider her a friend. I needed more time. I soon discovered that I wasn't indecisive. I was fickle.

The second I finished shouting the verse at Lila, my baby sister Grace began to cry like one of Tina's newborn pups—a safety net that swiftly drew Lila's attention away from my malicious tongue.

I didn't have time to slip into my Keds before heading out the door. Sliding on my butt down the rocky, limb-strewn slope of our yard resulted in burrs in my seersucker shorts, twigs in my hair, and splinters in my feet. In spite of all that, I began to roar with a slap-belly laughter, as I tumbled closer to the berm of Stage Road.

Horns blared, cars swerved, and profanities flew, picking up scattered debris. I waved, shouting, "Same to ya!"

"Watch it, kid! Ya tryin' to git yaself kilt?"

A coal black, skinny runt with braids that stuck straight out from the sides of her head like airplane wings screamed at me from the back of a rusted, red Chevrolet pickup truck, "Ya crazy cracker!"

"Better'n a black-eyed pea," I shouted back.

A single brake light shone through the Memphis heat, and I hurried back up the hill, praying to Mary, Joseph, and baby Jesus to save my skin.

When I looked back towards the house, Lila was standing like a monument on the front steps, her faded flowered apron shifting with the slight summer breeze. It was my favorite apron. It hung on a hook by the refrigerator, and whenever I would walk by it, I could smell the aroma of everything good: crisp fried chicken, bacon, Mrs. Butterworth's pancake syrup, barbecue sauce, and those damn fried apple pies. That's when I began to cry, sitting at the bottom of the hill, looking back at her formidable stance, and watching as she took up the corner of her apron and wiped at her eyes. When she turned to go back inside the house, she made sure to catch the screen door before it could slam shut.

# CHAPTER 25

My mama was a secretary for the plant manager at the Chromium Mining and Smelting Corporation in Memphis. Even in the hottest summer temperatures, she wore a suit every day. During summer vacation from St. Ann's Catholic School, I looked forward to watching her get ready for work. She teased her blond hair until it floated like a cloud on top of her head, creating tiny crevices that tempted wee bits of pollen. This morning she wore a pale yellow knitted jacket and skirt that loosely fitted her narrow body. Underneath the jacket she wore a white, satiny, sleeveless V-neck top. The pearls around her neck slid gently on her cameo skin whenever she moved her head. She looked like Grace Kelly in *To Catch a Thief*.

She had bought the suit last Saturday at Second Time Around. Mrs. Phaff always held back suits for my mother to try on, whenever the ladies who lived in Germantown tired of their unwanted clothes. They met Mrs. Phaff at the back alley of her shop, leaving their Cadillacs running while they lifted the car trunk and quickly handed Mrs. Phaff their "worn-only-a-few-times" designer suits, dresses, and frilly lingerie. Mrs. Phaff didn't particularly like being seen with any of them either, so she just as quickly gathered the garments in her arms and skedaddled back inside her shop, shaking her head at the sky and rolling her chestnut eyes.

Mama winked at me as she glided the cotton candy pink lipstick over her mouth. "Are you ready, Peanut?"

"Ready."

She flipped her wrist, pulling a Kleenex tissue from the box on top of the commode; she never liked the word toilet, and would scold us if she even heard the letter t escape our tongues. Then the ritual of folding the tissue in half, pressing it between her lips and removing it at the corners to avoid any lipstick stain on her fingers would begin; unfortunately, it always ended much too soon for me. The last sound I heard was the sound of a sweet kiss, followed by a melodic "ahhhhhh" escaping her vocal chords. She would wink again, throw me a kiss, and head out the back door, her step quickening to the honk of Mary's car out in the gravel driveway. We waved good-bye until we could no longer see each other's arms scooping up the air before I'd reluctantly go back inside, closing my eyes and remembering our house in Germantown, wishing Mama was dropping off her old clothes to Mrs. Phaff, rather than wearing someone else's hand-me-downs.

# CHAPTER 26

"**L**ucy," Lila bellowed, "child, git on in here now and eat your breakfast."

I wondered how Lila could be so sweet to me, after what I had said to her on Friday afternoon. I wondered if breakfast meant molded bread and spoiled milk. I wondered if she had told Mama what I said. I wondered what was going to happen to me if she had. Or, if I was lucky, maybe Mama would be on my side, wink, and say, "Way to go, Peanut." Yeah, and maybe it would snow before noon. I didn't care so much that I had recited the chant to Lila as much as I cared that Mama would want to know where I had heard it. Aunt Dodo had taught it to me last summer, but I never knew that I'd actually *say* it to someone one day. Something told me that it was wrong, but I said it to her after she had told me to stop acting like a child, after I'd stuck my tongue out at her. I had stuck out my tongue at her because she wouldn't let me have a second banana Popsicle. I love banana Popsicles. And I hate being called a child almost worse than anything else. I was more worried that Aunt Dodo would get in trouble, and Mama loved her so much. She loved me too, of course, but she'd forgive me. I wasn't so sure that she'd forgive Aunt Dodo. And now I wonder why Aunt Dodo would teach me the chant. When I first recited it I laughed, and yet I remember laughing in a way that I had never laughed before. I hadn't actually thought about that until just now. It was a nervous laugh, now that I think about it.

At the far end of the table sat *The Memphis Press-Scimitar*, the photo accompanying its front-page story staring at me like the picture of Jesus that hung on the wall in the principal's office at St. Ann's. Every kid before me and every kid to come after me would be rendered speechless by that picture, whenever called to Sister Mary's office. We all agreed that Jesus's eyes followed us wherever we looked, which was the main reason that we immediately admitted to whatever charge was leveled and agreed to never do it again, sitting on the very edge of the straight-backed wooden chair, anxious to bolt the very moment of being excused to return to class. And it was because of those eyes that we seldom repeated bad behavior. Now, at the very recollection of those eyes, I suddenly saw something very similar staring back at me from the morning paper.

Two young colored boys, twins, sixteen years old, had been missing for several months. Finally, after police and investigators and townspeople had searched the area and even made a plea to those outside the area, their bodies had been found. The newspaper had carried the story, and the headlines became more and more frightening every day. Some days another story became the front-page story, relegating the black youths' story to another page. They each had on pure white undershirts, and had the broadest smiles I've ever seen in my life—smiles that seemed to reach from ear to ear. Their eyes squinted, as if the photo had been taken in the bright sunlight. The headline read: "Missing Youths Discovered in Raleigh Ravine. KKK Suspected." With my middle finger and thumb, I flipped the paper off the table until it landed on the linoleum floor. I couldn't bear to look at those eyes again. I couldn't bear to read another word of that story. Out of sight, out of mind. Right? Yeah, sure. But even strewn on the floor, their eyes, like Jesus's, seemed to follow me. Their names, Thomas and Albert, stayed with me, even though I wanted them to leave. And why did their names bother me? They didn't seem like names of colored boys; all the colored boys I knew were named Leroy, Tyrone, or Willie. Like Thomas and Albert were names that belonged to white boys only.

I scooted out the chair next to my older sister's and plopped onto the thin, faded, blue-and-yellow-striped cushion. Caroline looked at me and rolled her eyes. I looked at her and stuck out my tongue. She always shrugged and looked away. It was a routine we engaged in every day, like brushing our teeth every morning and every night.

Every night when Mama would tuck us in bed, she always said, "Did you brush your teeth?" Sometimes we said, "Yes, ma'am," and then looked at each other and grinned. Every time we did this, we'd get up after Mama left the room and brush our teeth. Neither one of us could lie. Mama thought a lie was the absolute worst thing you could do, right along with stealing.

Mama was very particular about teeth. Before she and Daddy got married, a dentist told Mama she needed to have all her teeth removed and replaced with false teeth. Mama's Aunt Dodo and Uncle Herman were "appalled," Mama said, and they "one, two, three," took her to another dentist, who "saved her teeth." So, Mama was big on brushing twice a day and getting regular check-ups with Dr. Stevens. We knew that clean teeth and fresh breath were at the top of Mama's list of good hygiene, along with pure Ivory Soap, whole milk, and Quaker Oats.

Grace giggled, and Lila squeezed her plump little cheek. Even with Gerber bananas on her mouth and bib, she was the cutest baby ever. Even cuter than the Gerber baby. Our mama thought so, too. She even sent a picture of Grace to the Gerber people to let them see how cute she was, and let them know if they ever needed a substitute for their own Gerber baby, Grace would be a good fill in. She never received a letter back from Gerber. We just figured our letter must have been lost in the mail. Lila told Mama to stop buying Gerber, since they couldn't even write back and say "thanks, but no thanks." Mama just laughed, and kept right on buying Gerber peas, carrots, bananas, and peaches.

Every Monday morning Caroline and I would sit on the edge of our chairs, eating fast enough but not so fast that Lila would order us to slow down before we choked, waiting for the sound of the mail truck on our gravel drive. Then we would shout in unison like a couple of trained parrots, "I'm done!" before rushing to retrieve what we already knew were there.

Aunt Dodo and Uncle Herman mailed them from St. Louis every Friday: three postcards, each with two shiny dimes Scotch taped to the back and our names scratched across the front. The words "Shut Up" were written underneath the dimes. We laughed every single time we saw it, remembering that on our summer vacations we would spend two weeks with them, taking the train from Memphis to St. Louis. The conductor once shouted, "Shut up," to a man and woman who were fighting about how much money they had spent on their trip out West. Caroline and I laughed so hard that our mama said, "Shut up," and we all laughed and hurried out the dining car. When we told Aunt Dodo and Uncle Herman this story, they laughed and laughed until Uncle Herman started to gasp for air, which was actually not funny at all, since he has asthma.

Caroline and I each had a Daily Dime tin bank we'd received from Aunt Dodo and Uncle Herman, and we were supposed to put one dime in each week, "for a rainy day." When the dime was inserted into the thin slot, the bank would tell you the day and how much you had inside. Mine had a little pink piggy wearing a blue ribbon with daisies on it. Caroline's had a picture of a little girl at the beach, feeding ducks in the ocean. I've never seen another picture of ducks in the ocean, but I suppose the Kalon manufacturers thought it possible—one of those things you had to take on faith, like Jesus. Caroline and I put one of our dimes in the bank every week; but unlike Caroline, my rainy-day dime never stayed for long. Without fail, by mid-week I would pry open the slit with a butter knife and shake the bank upside down, until the dime fell with a sweet note onto the kitchen table. Caroline would just shake her head, and I'd stick out my tongue—my favorite response to her good-grief expressions. I hated that my bank was bent, but not enough to deter my future robberies. I once heard Mama say, "Flaws add character." I don't think she was talking about my bank.

"Hey Caroline, you wanna collect empty pop bottles along the road and go to Manny's for a soda?"

Monday mornings were the best time to find empty pop bottles at the base of our hill. The weekends in particular yielded a huge loot of glass bottles strewn along the gully, having been tossed by teenagers out the windows of their speeding cars.

Caroline put down her Nancy Drew mystery—she'd read most of them at least twice—and said, "Well, okay, let's go," like she was doing me a favor or something.

We walked along the gully, picking up every pop bottle we could find, looking first for broken tops before depositing them into the brown Piggly Wiggly grocery bag. We knew just about how many bottles could fit inside the bag before risking a busted bottom. We'd done that before, an event which always caused a "Damn," to escape from my mouth. That was the only time Caroline let my profanity slide by. She thought anyone who used profanity was just plain ignorant. I thought it refreshing, and even necessary in certain circumstances. A busted bottom paper bag was definitely a permissible circumstance.

We stopped off at the Texaco station and handed the overloaded brown bag to Fred, whose uniform was spotted with grease and oil that fell in a random pattern; it reminded me of a game of fifty-two card pickup, which I would surprise Caroline with whenever she beat me at rummy. The cards scattered here and there, always sliding underneath the sofa or behind the TV. Fred's green Texaco cap was tilted to the side, the Texaco Star assuring us that he could be trusted, or so Uncle Herman always said. "Phew," we sighed in unison.

"Well, here come my little bottle gatherers. How many did we find today?" he asked. Fred pulled a soiled, once-white handkerchief out of his back pocket, and slid it across his face and through each of his slippery fingers.

He pulled out Dr. Pepper bottles, grass-green 7Up bottles, and, my favorites—several of which I had lined up on my windowsill—those diminutive Coca-Cola bottles, with the red cursive writing that I tried over and over to emulate (I just love the way that word rolls off my tongue and into the heat of summer) on pieces of yellow construction paper. I like red and yellow together. It reminds me of ketchup and mustard, both of which I just adore.

"Looks like fourteen today, girls." Caroline and I smiled at each other—something we seldom did—as Fred opened the register and one by one put two dimes and one shiny copper penny in each of our hands. As he walked to the register, his back to us, we saw this morning's paper sitting on top of Fred's cluttered, rusty metal desk. The eyes of both of those twin colored boys were filled in with a black marker, and a slit had been made on each smile. Trailing from the slit made in their opened mouths were several red squiggly lines that reminded me of worms. Caroline saw it, too, and we moved closer to each other until the sweat beads rolling down our arms touched. It was magnetic. There was no breath coming from either one of us. We froze in place, and our eyes got as big as saucers—maybe even bigger.

"Well," Fred said, as he turned over the paper, "you two look like you've seen a ghost. Something wrong?" Even if we had wanted to say something, we couldn't. Neither one of us said anything. Fred just stood there looking at us, running his dirty handkerchief over his face and picking out dirt from under his fingernails. I wanted to move, but I couldn't. The only thing I was capable of doing was tugging on the hem of Caroline's shirt—hard.

"No, no, everything's fine. What could be wrong? Thanks, Fred," Caroline said, and we ran out of the odorous garage without looking back. We ran and we ran and we ran, until we got to Manny's, taking what seemed like forever to catch our breaths.

\* \* \*

Manny Applegate's drug store was located across the street of the busiest intersection on Stage Road.

"Well, good morning, my little darlings," Manny said with a grin that showcased his gold tooth. "My, you two seem quite out of breath this morning. You must have run all the way here today. Did you have a race?"

We just looked at each other and smiled and then smiled at Manny, shaking our heads in agreement, as if nothing was out of the ordinary. Caroline kicked my shin lightly and said, "Yes, sir, that's it. We raced each other over here."

"I see. Who won?"

"Oh," Caroline said, "it was a tie."

"Oh, I see. Well, since it was a tie, maybe I should treat both of you today. Take a seat at the counter, and Annie will be right with you. But before you do that, maybe Miss Lucy has some business to conduct."

"Holy cow, thanks Manny." And he gave us each a wink.

Manny was the only adult I knew who not only let, but encouraged kids to call him by his first name. He wasn't trying to be cool, he *was* cool, and we all loved him.

"So, Miss Lucy, ready to get *Open Road* out from behind the counter?"

Manny began what was to become the power of layaway plans for me, a twelve-year-old girl with aspirations to live out every Barbie outfit, except for her extravagant wedding gown. I had recently sworn never to marry. It seemed to me a nuisance, and saddled with too much heartache. I was so serious about my decision that I even wrote out my intentions on a sheet of notebook paper, asking Mama to put it in her safe deposit box. She said she would take it to the bank, and that she would only remove it on the day I got married—"Just for laughs." I assured her that she would need to find something else to laugh about. I said, "Ah, come on Mama, you know that once I make my mind up about something, I never change it." She just raised her eyebrows and said, "Oh, is that right? Well, we'll just have to see, now, won't we?"

"Ready," I said, and slapped down my remaining balance of eleven cents. Manny picked up each coin, penciled the amount on the index card that had my name at the top, and wrote zero on the balance line. I was not only happy to get *Open Road* out of layaway, but the zero balance opened yet another door for my next deposit to be put down on *Barbie Babysits*, which was another somebody I wanted to be some day, in addition to one day being a world traveler on the open road. I pictured myself wearing that coral-and-white striped apron with those cute little pockets, a picture of a little girl on one side and a little boy on the other. The names of the Good Girls were Betsy, Carrie, and Mary. The names of the Good Boys were Matty, Joey, and Billy. I often repeated these names; since there were three boys and three girls, it reminded me of a jump-rope rhyme. All it needed was a catchy ending, maybe even something that proved they were not good, but not really bad, either. Just normal. Even though I thought Barbie and I had parted ways, her every new adventure lured me back.

"Here ya go, sweets." When Manny bent down to retrieve the outfit, his blue polka-dotted bow tie bent with him, and I longed to reach down and straighten it.

"Thank ya ma'am." Manny treated every kid like a real customer, and we all thought we were his most prized possessions. "Thank you, sir," I replied with equal professionalism. Caroline just rolled her eyes, and took a seat at the soda fountain.

"I'll take a cherry Coke, and Lucy will have her usual," Caroline said to Annie. Annie never had a drop of tomato soup or a spot of hot fudge on her crisp, white apron with blue striped trim. I wanted to be her, too. And even though I didn't much care for Caroline assuming that I would have my usual, I never changed. As we sat at the sleek, shiny, stainless steel counter and whirled around and around on the bright orange vinyl stools until we got dizzy, I sipped every drop of that ice-cold bottle of Coca-Cola until there was nothing left but the sound of air through the straw.

# CHAPTER 27

"Your mama still have that fat nigger lady working in your house?" The Armeano twins jumped in front of us on our way home from Manny's, scaring us half to death. "She's not a nigger," Caroline shouted. "Her name's Lila, you moron."

"Who you calling a moron, nigger lover?"

Caroline scooped up a fistful of dirt and pebbles and hurled them at Tommy Armeano, who threw up an arm hoping to shield his face from her weapons. A tiny rock hit him on the cheek, breaking his skin a bit, the dark drop of blood pinpoint in size. His younger brother Robbie squealed and turned to run, shouting, "You bitches! We'll git you for this!"

"Just try," Caroline shouted.

"Yeah, just try," I said, knowing I wouldn't have said it with such conviction if Caroline hadn't been right there with me.

Caroline wasn't afraid of anything or anyone. It was times like this that I wanted to be her; I felt nothing bad could ever happen to me, as long as she was around.

"Come on, Lucy, let's go home," she said, and put her arm around my shoulders. She was only thirteen months older than me, but there were times we felt like twins. This was one of those times.

Walking past Fred's, we noticed our daddy's black Cadillac pulling away from the gas pumps and Fred waving goodbye with one hand, again wiping the sweat from his brow, only this time with his shirt sleeve. When he turned around, I saw the morning paper was folded and stuck inside his back pocket. When I went to wave to Daddy, Caroline pulled my arm down and took my hand in hers. I was both perplexed and calmed by her action. It was definitely not something I was used to, only wanted.

We walked in through the back door, because I still wasn't sure if Lila might jump out from behind a door, grab me, lock me in a closet, and throw away the key, and no one would ever see me again. I didn't want her to see me and use that switch that stung like a bee whenever she wielded it against my skinny legs. I could see her standing at the ironing board pressing sheets, sprinkling water from the Pepsi bottle, its cap having been poked with tiny holes. I never could figure out how she got that cap back on that bottle, or how it stayed in place. I'd have to ask her that one day, when she forgot about the nigger chant I sang to her.

"Like sands through the hourglass, so are the days of our lives." Lila and Caroline and I always watched *Day of Our Lives* together, but when Lila turned to look at me with squinted eyes to let me know that she hadn't forgotten, I decided to go to my room. I flung myself across the white chenille bedspread. I could hear Caroline playing with Grace, whose giggles swept through our tiny house like a babbling brook, making the faded rose wallpaper, the creaking floorboards and the cracked windows disappear for just a moment. In Germantown, Caroline and I didn't scoop up the pop bottles from alongside the highway, didn't have neighbors like the Armeano twins, and we didn't have a nigger ironing our sheets, smacking me with switches, or smelling up our kitchen with those damn, greasy, fried apple pies.

# CHAPTER 28

We spent the rest of the week poking around the dilapidated house that sat next to ours. Ever since we moved here in January, Caroline wondered how it got to be the way it was: empty, just waiting to be bulldozed to the ground, KEEP OUT and NO TRESPASSING signs randomly covering a window or the front door, or stuck in the overgrown lawn. It was unusual for Caroline to be so curious, especially about something that was run-down. Normally, that was my terrain. Every now and then, a feline would peek out through one of the various cracks it had available, as it scratched its flea-bitten shanks. Just looking at the house gave me the willies. But since Caroline had entertained my invitation on Wednesday to see if the pavement was hot enough to fry an egg on it (it was), I thought the least I could do was entertain her own curiosities. I think she'd been reading too many Nancy Drew mysteries, but I didn't have the nerve to say that to her. Maybe she wanted to be a detective when she grew up. Who knew? But she was convinced that the crumbling house was worth inspecting. As level-headed as she was, she was equally convinced that the house possessed ghosts—perhaps ghosts of children who used to live there. Again, it was so unlike Caroline to concoct these notions. I was a little baffled by all this, but like I said, I decided to entertain her thoughts. Every time she mentioned the ghosts I quickly changed the subject, even though I knew it was impossible. I mean, ghosts? I don't think so.

It was not unusual to see dilapidated houses in Raleigh, Tennessee. They were everywhere. It was never what you would call the bad side of town, but it wasn't the good side, either. And it certainly wasn't Germantown. Like our lives, it was somewhere in between the two. It kinda reminded me of the teeter-totter. Up, down, up, down, managing somehow to find a shaky balance, as long as your feet could touch the ground. Unlike Germantown, there weren't many lawyers or doctors. Instead, there were lots of ordinary folks, like plant workers, secretaries, gas station attendants, and drugstore clerks. It always seemed dirty, never shiny and polished like those copper pennies Fred gave us for our soda pop bottles, which didn't seem shiny at all, now. Not after what he had done to the newspaper pictures of those two colored boys. The luster had waned.

One time we walked to the back of the house, where a naked light bulb hanging from a frazzled cord shone eerily through a cracked window pane. Caroline wanted to get a closer look at the basement—why, I have no idea—but we soon found ourselves ankle-deep in muddy water. As we worked to keep each other from falling, Caroline said, "Look, Lucy." We both noticed that the bulb had gone out instantly, like candles blown out on a birthday cake. We quickly regained our footing and headed for home. But I knew she wouldn't forget about the house. She'd want to go back soon. And even when I tried to reason with her, which was a switch for us—she was always the one trying to reason with me—and told her that the bulb probably just went out on its own, she gave me a gentle, but firm push and said, "Hush up, Lucy." I squinted my eyes at her, but she had already walked ahead of me and didn't see it.

"I have a premonition," she said as she walked back to our house. "A feeling that I can't shake, Lucy. There is something about that house that in a really creepy sort of way, makes me feel connected to it somehow. I don't know what it is just yet, but I feel it." I didn't like the sound of that, and tossed it to the dry heat.

By the time Sunday evening approached, we eagerly set up the weekly ritual of being allowed to eat in the living room, placemats covering the scratched wooden coffee table in front of the sofa. It was the only day we were allowed to eat someplace other than at the kitchen table, and we looked forward to it with unbridled anticipation.

Every Sunday evening, Mama would phone in our dinner order to Willie Joe's BBQ, which was located right across the street from our house. Willie Joe's son, Lawrence—for some reason, everybody called him "the law," and then just laughed and laughed—would answer the telephone every time, and Mama would have to hold her hand over her mouth to keep from laughing. When we asked her about this, she said, "The way Lawrence says barbecue just tickles me something awful." She said the first syllable sounded like the baa of a sheep, not bar like a bar of soap. We didn't think it was that funny, but then we never actually heard Lawrence answer the telephone, either. Maybe if we had, we would have had to stifle a laugh, too.

Mama always timed the call perfectly. I don't know how she did that. But then, she seemed to do everything with perfection, even after leaving Germantown and moving to Raleigh. I wanted to be like her, too. Just like that bottle cap on the Pepsi bottle that Lila used to sprinkle our sheets, it was something else I added to my list of questions I needed answered—how did she seem to do everything to such perfection?

The aroma of the BBQ with so much sauce dripping from it that we often formed what looked like burgundy icicles on our chins as we ate every succulent bite wafted through the opened screen door, and Mama hummed the theme song from Walt Disney's *Wonderful World of Color*, never missing a beat. The coleslaw was smooth, rich, and creamy, like my red velvet skirt that I wore on Christmas, and the baked beans were served in little plastic cups, with a perfect crusted top waiting to be punched with the tines of our forks.

\* \* \*

The police siren woke Caroline and me, and we both popped up from the fetal position like a jack-in-the-box. We crouched below the window to the back yard, and the whirl of red lights lit up the woods behind our house. Tina poked her head out from inside her dilapidated dog house, barking loudly, and then turning back with panic. Caroline and I looked at each other in bewilderment. It was the first time we had seen Tina recoil at the sight of danger. And the only time we had ever seen a police car was when Fred had one hoisted up on steel planks inside the Texaco garage. Caroline and I held our breath, hoping the car didn't collapse on top of Fred as he worked on it from underneath.

Mama ran past our bedroom, turned for an instant to close our door, and said, "Just a minute," as the officer knocked with urgency at our back door. "Oh, my God," she whispered. I don't know if she was calling for God to help her with the police, or if she was embarrassed for the policemen to see her hair wrapped up in Scott tissue, something she did every night "to keep it in place." Maybe it was both. If it hadn't been the police at the door, I would have laughed. I always wanted to blow a light stream of breath at her sugary confection and watch it scatter to the winds, like a ripe dandelion. But not tonight.

"Maggie Moore?" the policeman asked, as he shone his flashlight in her face.

Mama squinted and said, "Yes?"

"We're looking for your husband. Is he here?"

"No. He's not here. We're not married, we're divorced. I don't know where he is. Has he done something? Has something happened?" Her voice quaked like a dying car engine and raced like a bee on the prowl. She didn't add the word 'wrong' at the end of something, nor did she add the words 'to him' after happened. We knew why. She didn't really care, which made us not care, either. And yet, just by her asking, I think that she did care. But at that moment, fear was the only thing any of us cared about, and it was an uninvited guest.

Suddenly I heard a sound from the far corner of the room where our bookcase— filled with Caroline's favorite book, *The Lonely Doll*, our Nancy Drew mysteries, and, next to my Barbie and her intoxicating clothes, my most prized possession, my copy of *To Kill a Mockingbird*, inscribed "To MY little Scout, Happy Birthday, Love, Mama"—was overshadowed by a looming figure.

Scout was my alter-ego, and could just possibly be at the top of my list of people I wanted to be when I grew up. I liked the way she, from time to time, snubbed Calpurnia, and I lived vicariously through her when she beat up on Walter Cunningham on the playground, something I wanted to do to the Armeano twins before I died.

"Be still."

Caroline nearly pushed me over when the soft, yet harsh voice met her acute hearing. Caroline's senses were always sharp. She could smell a cigarette miles away, hear a cicada all the way to Manny's, distinguish the difference between a lime and a lemon before it reached her tongue, and like a psychic, see, in sharp focus, impending danger lurking in the bushes. When Tina had her pups, we counted only six one morning, when the evening before there were seven. Caroline stood erect as a mannequin, closed her eyes, then walked towards the overgrown hillside, and said, "Here it is!" She reached inside the brush, and pulled out the whining little bastard.

"What the hell are you doing here?" My head snapped from the corner of the room, where I could make out a mere silhouette of my father, to my sister, whom I had never heard use profanity in my life, for she was much too sophisticated to resort to such ignorance. That's when I started to cry.

Caroline put her hand over my mouth with the first snivel, and I held it there, suddenly overwhelmed by the realization that I could barely breathe.

The knife's blade glistened with the rotation of the police car's blinking lights. I immediately thought of Scout in the movie, when she sneaked into Boo's backyard with Jem and Dill. When Jem climbed the rickety steps and pushed aside the crate to inch his way up to the window, there appeared a shadow that rendered Scout speechless. All she was able to emit was a single, barely audible sound. It was just enough to grab Jem's attention; the three sleuths bolted through the collard patch and under the fence to safety.

Our door slowly crept open (Mama hadn't completely pulled it to), and Caroline was focused on the police officer, still wielding his flashlight, which was blinding our mama. She shielded her eyes like she does when she forgets to wear her sunglasses. Caroline hadn't yet seen the knife in my father's callused hand. A tiny sound managed to seep through the fingers of our clasped hands, and she tightened her grip. I poked her in the side with my elbow, which startled her enough to flinch, turn, and gaze in bewilderment at the knife's sharp point and serrated edge. She matched my sound and simultaneously reached for one of my roller skates, hurling it like a spiraling football. Like my Beatles 45 "Paperback Writer" put on slow speed, its in-flight travel seemed to take forever before the knife escaped from my father's hand and landed on its tip in front of us. Our father instantly plummeted to the floor, falling like a stiff board; his head hit the linoleum hard, and the roller skate ricocheted off the makeshift cinder block bookcase and soared through the window like a shooting star. My prized collection of diminutive Coca-Cola bottles fell from the windowsill like bowling pins.

# CHAPTER 29

Before Mama and Daddy got a divorce, they hosted the most refined social gatherings in Germantown. They were never called anything as plain and nondescript as "a party." Mama would call Betty Stephenson at Lowenstein's several weeks before the social event, to arrange an appointment—she never, never entertained the thought of repeating a table design—to coordinate table linens and choose magnificent centerpieces. My very favorite was a cut-glass crystal Waterford bowl that Mama crowded with white peonies and red roses, blue verbena cascading around the bowl's rim like a wedding veil. Every flower came from Mama's garden. This arrangement was to celebrate our annual Fourth of July lawn party.

Herend's Rothschild Bird tableware set the table, with Tiffany's Audubon sterling silver flatware, both of which were given to Mama when her parents were killed in a car accident, right after she graduated Our Lady of Sorrows. Place cards had a tiny embossed American flag in the upper left corner. The cards were held in place on Herend leaf place card holders that were adorned with a white porcelain rose. Alongside the Saint-Louis crystal sat a miniature sterling silver frame that held a crisp white sheet of paper from Mama's Crane & Co. stationery, with "Yankee Doodle Dandy" scattered about the paper in red and blue. I asked Mama to make an extra one of these little gifts for me, because I thought one would look perfectly-scaled next to my chorus line of Coca-Cola bottles. Her lagniappes were looked forward to almost or more than the evening's fare of barbecued oysters, grits, sweet corn with tomato and avocado relish, apple slaw, and watermelon slices on the veranda.

Mama greeted her guests dressed in a sleeveless fuchsia and lime floral printed Lilly Pulitzer shift, white ballet shoes, and Chanel No. 5. Daddy wore a pair of sky blue seersucker trousers and a white golf shirt, his tanned feet tucked into polished penny loafers.

"Welcome, welcome, come on in," Daddy said. He kissed each lady on the cheek and slapped the back of each one of his buddies, leaving the ornately-adorned front door of our antebellum home open for the next guest. When his best friend and business partner Scooter walked in, Daddy shook his hand, leaned in, and whispered in his ear, "We got us another one, didn't we?" I suddenly felt a chill in the warm summer air that hadn't been there before, an odd chill that I'd never felt before, and didn't know why. I wondered what he meant by the words "another one." *Another what*, I thought? Then they both stifled a laugh, but not until Scooter said, "Correction, partner. We got us two." That was when I knew where the chill came from; it was something instinctive, telling me that something was wrong. Something I didn't want to think about. But I couldn't quite put my finger on it. Then Scooter's wife Peaches (I never knew their real names) startled me when she blurted out of nowhere, "My, my, Miss Lucy. Don't you look like a little doll baby in that sundress." Doll baby? Are you kidding me? When she nudged Daddy and Scooter, they seemed as jumpy as I did on the last day of school when I rearranged the things on Sister Agnes's desk. (She was so organized that it drove us all crazy. So I turned her rabbit bookends the opposite direction, moved her vase of roses from her garden to the opposite side of her desk, turned her pencils in her pencil holder upside down so the erasers were at the bottom, and rearranged her stack of books from being perfectly lined up to a zigzag pattern.)

"Oh, Lucy," Daddy said with surprise. "I didn't see you. You sneaked up on me, didn't you?" He pulled me to him and hugged me, and winked at Peaches. Then Scooter cleared his throat. I was more than a little uneasy, but didn't exactly know why.

Mama and Peaches were best friends and cheerleaders in high school. Peaches dated Scooter, who was the captain of the basketball team, and Mama dated Daddy, who was the quarterback of the football team. Every Friday night after a home game, the four of them would meet at Reggie's Burgers and Dogs, Mama and Daddy in his red Cadillac convertible. One time, Mama's pompoms flew out of the convertible; Daddy quickly made a U-turn, sped back to the scene of the crime, and gathered up the pompoms, sailing them back inside the car. Mama said he was her hero from that moment on. Even though I liked this story, I always thought it was just a bit weird that Mama's idea of a hero was someone who would recover her pompoms.

I loved Daddy more than anything in the world, but I thought a hero should be more than that.

Caroline and I loved to hear Mama tell stories about her and Daddy when they were in high school. She told the best stories ever, as we sat in the window seat with our feet propped up on the edge of the red gingham cushion, sipping Coca-Cola.

Last Christmas, after all the gifts had been opened, Mama handed Caroline and me a crisp, white envelope—the one that had her initials engraved on the back flap, in heavy black cursive lettering. She had sealed the tip of the flap with hunter green sealing wax, making an impression of a Christmas tree in the center of the wax. Mama winked and grinned with such sadness that I could have cried. I snapped out of my reverie when she said, "Merry Christmas." Inside was a typed story, the one that Caroline and I loved most of all the stories Mama told us—one we'd asked her to re-tell so many times we could almost repeat it verbatim, like so many parts of To Kill a Mockingbird.

Caroline and I mimicked each other, holding the paper close to our heart, like Mama did when she held Grace. A tear slowly fell down Mama's cheek and what happened next will be emblazoned in my mind until the day I die—I'm certain of it. Daddy, who hadn't spoken for what seemed like hours, stood up, walked over to Mama, wiped away the tear, and touched the briny note to his parched lips. And then he just kept on walking, stopping for a brief moment to look at Grace before heading out the front door. Caroline and I looked at each other with a mix of confusion and astonishment. He didn't say anything. He just kept walking. For just a split second after he touched Mama's cheek, she flinched; it was the most alarming thing we had ever seen in our lives. She flinched like she couldn't stand his touch on her cheek, like she was scared, sickened, and relieved, all at the same time. And while we didn't know it at that moment, what had just happened signaled the beginning of the end.

## "Father Joe's Cowboy Boots"

*After we won the championship game against St. Joe's Cavaliers, we all, as usual, peeled away from the field, gravel flying, and drove in a mad rush to Reggie's. Father Gladsby pulled in, and we all suddenly turned our attention to him in disbelief. It was the first time we'd ever seen him, or any priest for that matter, without his collar. He had on a pair of Levi's, pointed-toe lizard cowboy boots, and* a very handsome chocolate brown V-neck cashmere sweater, with a simple white undershirt underneath. Marlena Swingers said, "Wow." But then she always said, "Wow," whenever she saw a handsome guy, so none of us really paid any attention to her, except Tommy Dillon, the Baptist preacher's son, who said, "Marlena! He's a priest." "So?" Marlena said. "He's still a man." Then she walked away, shaking her right hand, and shouting, "Phew!"

Nancy Ketchums couldn't see a thing—even if it was right in front of her face—without her thick, pointed-frame glasses. But when she was at Reggie's, she often took them off. She hated wearing them. She hated her red, frizzy hair, too, but most of all, she hated those glasses. When she got out of her boyfriend's car, she flung the glasses in the back seat, and propped herself against the trunk, squinting at the night air, using her keen hearing to pick up the conversations that melded together. The cacophony of sounds made her seem part of the fanfare.

Father Gladsby walked around the parking lot, congratulating the players on their win against St. Joe's. All of a sudden Nancy teeters up to him, waving furiously, shouting, "Hi there, Father!" Then, before anyone could stop her, she slips on a fry and skids right into Father. He loses his balance, and the next thing you know, his pointed-toe, lizard cowboy boots are sticking straight up to Heaven. Thank God Daddy was only inches away. His quarterback swiftness caught Father Gladsby just before he landed on the ground. The music suddenly stopped; Reggie ran out of the kitchen, arms flailing, and shouted, "Oh, my God!" Everyone, including Marlena, looked at Reggie. Father Gladsby said, "Precisely, Reggie. Ya got any burgers left, or did this crew eat all of them already?"

Everyone laughed and quickly helped Nancy to her feet, her loafers wearing the remains of the squashed fry, and Reggie went inside to grill Father's burger just the way he liked it, with all the fixings.

Christmas, 1965
Love, Mama

# CHAPTER 30

"Oh, Miz Maggie," Lila said, shaking her head. She pulled out her flowered cotton handkerchief, which she kept snug inside her dress belt, and wiped at her tears. Her black housedress made her look even darker than usual, but the tears that fell were like the clear, cool raindrops that dripped from the roof's gutters outside my bedroom window after a morning shower, the honeysuckle's sweet fragrance pulling me to it like a sleepwalker. Mama liked Lila, and the fact that Lila was crying right along with Mama made me feel even worse about that damned little chant I sang to her the week before.

Lila was shucking corn, the husks forming a carpet at the base of her splayed legs. "I do declare. And right in front of them little girls. Sweet Jesus." It was times like these that I had to fight the urge to dislike her. I mean, when someone likes your mama and your sisters, well, it's just plain difficult not to like them back. But I wasn't giving in just yet; I was still holding out, for what I didn't know exactly.

Mama sat across from her at the kitchen table, the toe of her spiked black patent heel tap-tap-tapping on the floor. Grace was still sleeping softly in her crib, and Caroline and I were sitting cross-legged on the living room sofa.

"Hey, Caroline, wouldn't it be great if Mama could appear on that show? What was it called again? You know, the one she told us she used to watch when we were real little, because it always made us laugh."

"What was the name of it, Caroline?"

"Caroline!"

"Oh, Lucy, I can't think about that right now."

"Please, Caroline. I have to talk about something funny."

"Oh, okay. I think it was called *Queen for a Day*. Good grief, Lucy."

92

"Yeah, that was it. *Queen for a Day*. What was the name of the announcer? Was his first name Jack or Jeff or . . ."

"Yeah, I think so. Yeah, it was Jack, and his last name was Bailey, wasn't it?"

"Yeah, that's right. Jack Bailey. Mama said he would skip and dance around the stage and introduce each of the contestants. I think each one talked about their problems or heartaches—something like that, didn't they?"

"Yeah, something like that."

Mama was talking to Lila, and Caroline interrupted my next question.

"Lucy, please, I want to hear what Mama is saying."

"Caroline, wouldn't it be great if Mama could go on that show? After what happened, I bet she'd win and get to wear a crown and a robe and carry a bouquet of roses. That's what the winner got to do, right? And, they got their wish granted, too, didn't they?"

"Caroline?"

"Yes, Lucy, they got their wish granted. Now would you rush, please?"

I pointed my finger at Caroline, pretended to clap my hands, and said, "Would *you* like to be queen for a day?"

"Lucy, please stop it, okay?"

I rested my head on the back of the sofa, clasped my hands, and faintly recalled the panning of the audience and the bright lights, Jack Bailey skipping and dancing around the stage.

"Caroline? Caroline?" She held up her right index finger to silence me.

"Listen," she said. Mama was talking in a low voice. Caroline and I edged forward and strained to listen.

"When I talked with Mark this morning, he said, 'Don't worry about anything, Maggie. Take as much time as you need. Let me know if you need anything.' Oh, Lila, he's so nice. So kind. We've had such a good time together these last few months. I'm growing fond of Mark, and I think he feels the same about me. It seems that everyone I've met since the divorce is more comfortable to be with than people I've known my whole life—or thought I knew, anyway."

"Mark?" Caroline and I whispered to each other.

"Who's Mark?" I whispered.

"I don't know," Caroline replied. "Shhhh."

"Caroline? Lucy? Are you two doing okay in there?"

"Yes, Mama," we said, like a couple of mynah birds.

"Are you sure?"

"Yes, Mama," Caroline reassured her.

After a few minutes, Caroline said, "Aren't we, Lucy?"

"Sure," I said, and we reached for each other's hands, holding them with a firm grip. Then, as if on cue, I whispered, and without knowing why, "Maggie and Mark sitting in a tree, k-i-s-s-i-n-g. First comes love, then..." and Caroline jabbed me so hard in the side that I almost doubled over. And even though we were both frozen stiff with fear, we laughed.

# CHAPTER 31

"Why Peanut, you look as if you are in deep thought about something," Mama said. She scooted in next to me at the kitchen table, the morning paper tucked underneath her arm.

I was looking through one of Caroline's fashion magazines, which never really held any interest for me whatsoever, as I finished up my breakfast of Cheerios and sliced bananas. Caroline and I had just started Vacation Bible School.

"Mama," I said, "ever since we started the girls' softball team at school last year and I saw Sister Theresa make that home run, I have been giving some thought recently to becoming a nun." I wasn't sure about the convent part of the equation, but I thought it was worth my time to consider it. Sister Theresa was my most favorite teacher. She taught English, and her cursive writing was as graceful as the honeysuckle, as it intertwined its branches throughout the vine, waving with the slight summer breeze. Her black tunic kicked up a slight stream of dust, and her arms spread wide as she stomped on home plate to announce her triumph, looking like Jesus himself on the cross, but with a look of victory and not one of pain and resignation. And yet, Father Tim always said that in Jesus's pain we experienced victory. Not exactly an easy thing to figure out.

Not looking up from my magazine, fearing that Mama would look at me like I had horns growing out of my head, I said, "I'd like to take Sister Theresa out to lunch one day, after inviting her to go with us to the convent, that is. I think I might want to be a nun when I grow up. I mean, she gets to read books to us every day and score home runs on the diamond." I made this proclamation with the speed with which I jumped into bed every night from the foot. I never jumped from the side for fear of encroaching ghosts, or worse yet, one of those gigantic water bugs that sometimes made their way into the house.

Suddenly, as if I had actually sprouted horns, I looked up to see Mama, Lila, Caroline, and even Grace frozen in place, like mannequins in Lowenstein's windows. Lila's brows were wrinkled and her hands were in place on her hips. Caroline's orange slice seemed to float in the air, just outside her opened mouth, and Grace even stopped beating her tray.

I couldn't decide whether I should cry from sheer embarrassment or grin from ear to ear with pride and certainty, like I had just discovered the cure for cancer. I was leaning towards the first until Mama said, "Well, then it shall be, my dear. I'll call Sister today and make the arrangements." At that moment, it was as if the play button had been pushed, and everyone went back to what they were doing. I simply beamed, and went back to reading an article that said your hair will shine more if you put mayonnaise on it. *What?* I tossed the magazine aside, grabbed a piece of paper, and began to draw little doodles of myself in full nun's habit.

# CHAPTER 32

After Mama and I went on a tour with Sister Theresa of the Sisters of Sorrows Convent, I began to feel real, true sorrow for them, rather than the awe I had felt earlier. First of all, there was very little talking; what little there was went on in whispers. Mama kept putting her finger up to her lips to remind me that we were in a convent, and I needed to show respect. Sister Theresa would just smile at me, encouraging me to ask as many questions as I wanted to—after the tour was completed. Every nun we passed in the wide corridors held her head low, most of them fingering the giant beads that hung from their tunics. There were crucifixes everywhere, and Jesus's eyes seemed to follow me wherever I went, almost like he was warning me—against what, I couldn't quite decide. The stained-glass windows seemed to catch the sun's rays and possess its brightness, making me shudder in their strength. The heavy stone walls and thick tiled floors carried the shushing sounds of the sisters' tunics, and the dense wooden doors closed with a deafening thud. I suddenly felt the urge to use the bathroom, but decided that I'd wait until we got to Steak 'n Shake. When we got there, I was certain I'd ask those waitresses how long it took to become a Steak 'n Shake waitress, because six years seemed like an eternity—especially six years of silence. That sealed the deal. Our family would not have a nun after all, because there was no way that I could ever be silent.

# CHAPTER 33

On Monday morning, Lila walked through the back door, her arms burdened with a stack of magazines and a red school folder.

Ever since Mama hired Lila to take care of Grace during the day, and Caroline and me when we came home from school every day, she was like a thorn in my side. And then there were times when she wasn't. Summers were even more trying, since we saw her every day, all day long. I never could stop thinking about those colored boys that Daddy talked about in his letter. I kept wondering what it all meant exactly, because there were so many details that had not yet been filled in, and every time I saw Lila I thought about showing her Daddy's letter, for just a split second. And every time, I stopped. We had been reading about the KKK in school, and I still couldn't get my head wrapped around so much of it. It seemed that every white person was mad at every colored person, and every colored person was mad at every white person. And yet Lila was taking care of us, so how could she be all bad just because she was colored? It was all too complicated and too worrisome for me to think about. It was a mystery that had yet to be solved. Even Nancy Drew would have a hard time with this one.

Scooter and Peaches had moved away, but no one knew where they went. Their names, along with Daddy's and some other prominent and not-so-prominent businessmen in town, were mentioned in whispers and in the newspapers, but there was no proof that they had done anything wrong. Only speculation. Even Fred's name was mentioned, which we weren't surprised by at all. I guess he couldn't be trusted, after all.

Mama constantly reminded us that it was none of our concern, which only complicated matters. Of course it was our concern! Daddy had been implicated in a crime that no one had yet named. Maybe there was no name for what was being reported. I once heard someone say the word heinous. Even when I looked up the definition in the dictionary, it still didn't cover it all. I don't think a word had yet been invented for what they had done to those colored boys. Sometimes people looked at us funny. Sometimes they crossed the street to avoid looking at us; at other times, they were overly kind. You can sense that kind of thing. It's like trying to cover up a blackhead with makeup; it just shows up even more.

"Good evenin', Miss Lucy. Are ya havin' a nice vacation, chile? How'd ya like the convent? Did ya like the cake I baked yesterday? I knowed your favorite was chocolate, so I made sure to make a chocolate cake with chocolate icin'."

"Yes ma'am," I said. "Thank you. It was delicious. The best chocolate cake I ever had. What 'cha got there?"

Ever since Mama began to go out with her friends on Monday nights, Lila started to stay with us until she got back home. I had made the decision to try to like her, even though I tried very hard not to let her know. I still wasn't sure that I wanted to be friends with her, but like vine-ripe tomatoes, she had begun to grow on me. I can't say just why for certain, but Daddy's letter might have had something to do with it.

"It's past copies of the *Catholic Bulletin*. I keeps 'em all, and thought you'd might like to read 'em," she said with an exhalation of breath, as she plopped the stack beside me.

"Oh, is that right?" I said, not looking up from the book I was reading.

"Wait a minute," I caught the odd thing about what she'd said. "What would you be doing with a stack of *Catholic Bulletins*?"

"Well, you didn't think you was the only person who was Catholic now, did you?"

"But, you're, you know," I stammered and stopped. Just when I thought I had begun to piece things together on most fronts, it was Lila who was the constant, who would intervene and mix things up again, like a tossed salad. I found myself both grateful and annoyed at the same time. Instead of stopping her in her tracks, I opened wide the door to her every time.

"Yes?"

"You know."

"Know what?"

"You know," I repeated, and looked at her with wide eyes, as I scanned her height.

"Oh, you mean 'cause I's a colored woman?"

"Well, yeah," my stammering continued. I suddenly realized that I sounded like what my mama would call poor white trash, and I just as suddenly gasped, much to my surprise, and even embarrassment. Lila could push my buttons in ways that no one else could, yet I found myself looking forward to the next challenge that she would put to me.

"Why, honey chile, you think only white peoples can be Catholic?"

"Well, I guess. I mean, I never really thought of it before, but yeah, I guess. I mean I never saw a colored person in church before, and we don't have any colored children in our school, and come to think of it, I didn't see any colored nuns at the convent."

"Well I'll be, chile. I do declare. Is that a fact now? You didn't see one colored sister at the convent? Well, what do ya think of that?"

"Well I don't really know what to think about that. What do you think about it?"

It was the first time that I'd ever asked Lila what she thought about anything. I was for reasons I didn't yet know, suddenly frightened; so much so that when she patted me on the top of my head, I flinched in the same way that Mama did when Daddy lightly touched her that last Christmas morning.

"Well, I guess I don't rightly thinks much about it, 'cept that it just ain't right. It's actually just plain wrong. I mean, do *you* think it's right?"

"Do I think what's right?" I frowned, not really knowing what the question was that she asked. I was beginning to feel a little confused.

"Does you think it's right that there ain't no colored people in your church, or in your school, or that there ain't no colored women at the convent?"

"I guess I never really thought about it," I said, knowing full well that I didn't think colored people should be allowed to go to our church or our school, and certainly that colored women shouldn't be allowed to go to the convent. But for just a split second, I did wonder why I felt that way. I just did. Besides, I didn't think a colored woman would look right wearing a black tunic, except that the white wimple would be a nice background for a black face. I shut my eyes tight, grimaced, and shook my head with equal determination. When I opened my eyes, Lila said, "Well, what do ya think?"

I bit my lower lip, grabbed my book, and headed out the door to sit on the front porch, to get away from a conversation that was bothering me more with every passing moment.

# CHAPTER 34

As the sun began to set, I headed back inside the house.

Lila had gathered up the stacks of *Catholic Bulletins* from the kitchen table, their spines in perfect alignment, and sitting in the center of the table, like a priceless crown, was the red school folder that she had brought with her earlier. We had been so wrapped up in our troubling discussion that I had completely forgotten about the folder. Well, at least it was troubling for me. I was dying to know what was inside, but instead acted like I couldn't care less. Caroline had gone to spend the night with her friend Elizabeth, Mama wasn't home yet, and Grace was sleeping. Suddenly, the house seemed very quiet, and I wished that I was anywhere but here.

I could hear the whirl of the fan, and Lila was humming "Amazing Grace" in the kitchen, the aroma of her crispy fried chicken wafting through the doorway. Damn, I wished she wasn't such a good cook.

In front of the red folder was a steaming hot, fried apple pie. Lila walked into the dining room with an ice-cold glass of milk, set it beside the plate, and winked. I smiled a toothless smile, and thanked her. I had never before seen her wink. She patted me on top of my head and said, "You's welcome, Sweet Pea," and walked back to the kitchen to tend to her fried chicken. She had never before called me Sweet Pea, either. But I was surprised to discover that neither the wink nor the endearment bothered me, which did bother me.

I peeked around the corner to make sure she had disappeared into the kitchen before I opened the folder, careful not to make a single noise. The essay was titled, "What I Want To Be When I Grow Up," by Lila Marks. Grade 5 was printed below her name in pencil, and the date: September 10, 1920.

With every bite of that dripping fried apple pie, I read the neat penmanship of a ten-year-old little colored girl. At one point, I closed my eyes and tried to imagine what Lila looked like as a little girl. I had actually never thought about her in any other way than how she looked since she came to work for my mama. I tried to scale down her frame, remembering how Alice in *Alice in Wonderland* had suddenly shrunk when she drank the contents of the bottle, and a vision of a tiny black Lila made me giggle. I suppressed the chuckle, not wanting the grown-up Lila to peer around the corner. And as I continued to read, I found that with every page, tears began to form at the corners of my eyes. I suddenly decided that maybe, just maybe, I'd be her friend. And that maybe, just maybe, we were more alike than I wanted to admit.

"What I Want To Be When I Grow Up"
By: Lila Marks
Grade 5
September 10, 1920

When I grows up I wants to be a nun. I wants to be a nun 'cause ever Sunday when I goes to church, they all come in together and gets to sit in the very first pew. I always sits in the last pew with my mama and daddy. It gets a little lonely sometimes. I don't have no brothers or sisters. My mama almost died when I was born, and she couldn't have no more chilren. Sometimes she gets to huggin' on me so that I can't hardly breathe. Last year for my birthday, my auntie Ruby gave me a little doll that was dressed like a nun. There was even a gold cross necklace that was tied round her neck. The nuns who comes to church ever Sunday are white. And my new doll is white, but since only her face shows, I painted it black so's I could see what I would look like as a nun. I never saw a black nun before. After I got my doll for my birthday, I got a white pillowcase from the linen closet and pressed it around my face to see what I would look like as a nun. I think I looked pretty. I hope God thinks so too. I can't wait to be the first black nun ever.

I wants to be a nun 'cause they gets to live in a pretty house that has very pretty very green grass 'round it, with very pretty rose bushes. They gets to teach little chilren at school, and they gets to play softball in the summertime. They don't get called names. Everybody treats them nice. Sometimes I gets called nigger child. They never has to worry about what to wear, either. But one thing I would change would be that they could wear jewelry. I likes necklaces and bracelets. Maybe God will let me wear lipstick one day. My mama wears very bright red lipstick and it makes her look pretty. I also likes her red sparkly earrings. But mostly I wants to sit in the first pew 'cause I has a hard time hearing the priest. I only hears out of one ear. That happened when I was born. Plus they look really important sittin' in the first pew. I wants to look important too. I wants to know why they ain't any colored nuns. Maybe one day when I gets to be a nun I can axe the priest. He might know. He knows everthin'.

**THE END**

# CHAPTER 35

magining life without Caroline or Grace is as inconceivable as imagining life without Mama or Daddy. And yet Daddy is gone. He won't ever be back, and that is as certain as my knowing after I read Lila's fifth grade essay that we would be friends forever. It was that quick, and still that perplexing. Something had changed. Too much had changed in such a short time. It made me as dizzy as the times Caroline pushed me in circles in the tire swing in our back yard. The more I begged her to stop, the more I asked her to keep doing it. Like I said, perplexing.

After I read Lila's essay, she came out of the kitchen with a plate for each of us. Fried chicken, butter beans, okra, and piping hot cornbread. Before I drenched the cornbread with a generous pat of butter, I looked at her for the first time. Really looked. Her skin was as smooth as silk, no imperfections. Her black hair had tiny bits of gray, like pollen, sprinkled evenly throughout, which gave her an air of distinction. Her earlobes held a tiny pair of ruby earrings. When I asked her about them, she told me that her mother left them to her when she passed away, just two days after her father was killed in a boating accident. She said what killed her mama was pure grief. I didn't even know that her parents had died. But then, I'd never asked. While I was surrounded by friends at school, Father Tim and Sister Theresa, and Mama, Caroline, Grace, Aunt Dodo, and Uncle Herman, Lila had no one. "I has all of you," she said when I told her that I was sorry that she was all alone. "And I has my church family. And most important, I has the Lawd." And for the first time since I met her, I was ashamed. I was sorry that I had not been nicer to her, had not asked her about herself—ever—and sorry that I had ever spoken one word of that chant to her.

And yet, there were still times when I hadn't completely made up my mind whether to like Lila, feel sorry for her, or completely decide once and for all that no matter what, I wasn't ever going to like her. I hated that we were alike. But in a way that I didn't really understand, I also liked that we were alike. We had been studying about conflict and resolution in stories that year in English class, and I was somewhere between the two in deciding what role, if any, Lila would play in my life. I wanted to resolve our conflicts, because Father Tim once talked about how people shouldn't stay mad at each other for long. He said, "Really, who wants to stay in that spot?" He was right, of course. But trying to figure it all out was as confusing to me as trying to figure out how that pop bottle cap stayed on when Lila sprinkled our sheets before ironing them.

Mama once said that I thought too much, and she is probably right. I do. But I can't help it. There are still so many things that are yet to be resolved. We know that Mama divorced Daddy because of what he did, but she doesn't know that we know the 'why'. And she still doesn't know about the letter. I think what we want most is for her to tell us what Daddy did. We need to hear it from her. Until she tells us, we will never be okay with it. Until she tells us, we can't move past it. Where I talk all the time about everything, my mama never talks about Daddy. It is as if he never existed. And while I understand that, I don't understand it, either. If Lila could forgive me for shouting that awful chant and love me just the same, how come Mama can't forgive Daddy? But then, there really is no comparison, is there? Caroline has become almost as closed-lipped about what was going on in her mind. I often find her in that dead stare of hers, when nothing—not even a train wreck—can bring her out of her trance. One time when she was staring out into the blue yonder, I jumped in front of her, wildly flailing my arms like a crazy person, and she didn't even flinch. I don't think she's crazy or anything like that, I think I just get on her nerves, and she pretends I'm not there. And then out of the blue, she'll ask me to go to Manny's for a soda. It's baffling, but I rush to her side whenever she calls, like an ant to sugar.

# CHAPTER 36

"What was that noise," the officer asked, with the urgency of a breaking news story that suddenly interrupted one of our favorite TV shows?

"What noise?" Mama said.

"Excuse me, ma'am, but we'll need to come inside," the officer commanded.

Both officers pushed open the screen door, drawing their guns and pointing them in every direction, just like Matt Dillon on *Gunsmoke*.

As they entered our room, surveying the dishevelment, Daddy regained consciousness and shook his head. The officer said, "Freeze!" Daddy looked into the open barrel of the policeman's revolver. We hadn't seen Daddy since last Christmas Day, except when I saw him at Nick's window and when he was leaving Fred's.

Caroline and I were scooped up by the other officer like a couple of rag dolls and tossed into Mama's spread arms, like he was passing off a football to a quarterback.

"Are you okay?" she asked. She looked from one of us to the other, checking all appendages to make sure that we weren't bleeding or bruised or maimed in any way.

"We're fine, Mama," Caroline answered for both of us. I was relieved, since for the first time in my life, I couldn't find my voice.

The officers were helping Daddy to his feet, handcuffing him, and reading him his rights. It was a scene right out of a movie, only this was real life. It was really happening to us.

"Maggie," Daddy shouted with uncharacteristic ferocity, "I'm sorry. I'm so sorry. But you must know that what I did was the right thing to do. In your heart, I'm sure you agree with what we're all trying to do. We must all do what we can to protect our children from them niggers. We can't have them niggers mixing with our kind. Them boys got what they deserved."

Caroline and I looked at each other in disbelief. What Daddy was saying was nothing like what he wrote in his letter. Maybe he *was* crazy, after all.

Mama put her hands to her ears and shook her head violently.

Caroline shouted, "Stop it, Daddy! How could you say things like that? Do you know that we are loved and taken care of by a colored lady every day after school, who helps us with our homework and who watches TV with us and who plays with Grace? She's the nicest person *ever*. How would you like it if somebody decided that we weren't good enough to live? Who are you? Why did you come back here? I don't want to know you anymore. I don't want you to ever come back!"

Caroline was shouting so loudly and so convincingly that the picture suddenly became too clear in my mind. Like a Nancy Drew mystery, all the i's had been dotted and all the t's had been crossed. Like it or not, our daddy had done something so unspeakable, so despicable, that it was separate from us in every way—but connected to us in every way, too. I was acutely aware that if it was indeed all true, it would be necessary for me to somehow right his wrongs; I vowed right then to do just that, any way I could, even if it took me the rest of my life to do it.

"That's enough, Mr. Moore," the officer said, as he led Daddy to the police car, his palm on Daddy's head to make sure he didn't hit the top of the cruiser—as if any of us cared.

"You're sick. What you're doing is sick. It's wrong. I don't even know who you are!" Mama shouted, as she hovered over us like a mother bird protecting her nest of eggs.

Caroline and I looked at each other in both bewilderment and acceptance, but neither of us said anything more. The officer held up his hand to stop Mama from approaching any closer and said, "Ma'am, we'll take care of everything from here. He won't bother you anymore."

Mama moved us closer to her and farther away from Daddy, as he blew us a kiss from inside the police car. He was in the back seat, a grilled partition separating him from the officers in the front. We seemed to know instinctively that we didn't want him to touch us, any more than Mama wanted us to be touched by him. I looked into his eyes, and saw an emptiness that I'd never seen before—an emptiness that matched the decay and void that permeated the rooms of the recently-condemned house next to ours, that now held only scattered broken glass and scurrying mice, looking for any scraps of crumbs, only to find nothing. There never was anything there. It was always empty. I think that Caroline wanted something to be there. She wanted to find a story, but there just wasn't one. Like I wanted to believe that Daddy hadn't done those awful things, but it just wasn't true. He had done them. And having done them, they could not be undone. Some things *are* exactly what they appear.

# CHAPTER 37

A few weeks before the start of the new school year, it was close to dusk when we heard the crackle from the fire and saw the sparks from its flames rise to the evening sky. The saffron yellow and burnt umber reminded me of Van Gogh's olive trees that we looked at the year before, in a slide show during art class at school.

Mama had finally told us about Daddy, even though we had already figured out most of it for ourselves. We had connected the many pieces of the puzzle until they all fit, but hearing it from her made the puzzle complete. This particular evening, she had invited lots of her friends from work, their kids, and her boss, Mark, to a cook-out in our back yard. Mark's richly-tanned skin seemed to meld with the colors of the setting sun. His dark brown, tousled hair seemed to be well kept, and his pleated khakis were expertly pressed. He wore a navy collared golf tee, and had a cherry red cotton sweater tied around his neck. If he suddenly boarded a shiny white sailboat, I wouldn't have been surprised. I looked and looked for a monogram on his golf shirt or sweater, but I didn't find one anywhere. That brought both an unexpected and relieved smile to my face. At that moment, he winked at me, and I was as assured as I had ever been that maybe, just maybe, I could stop worrying about everything. That maybe we all could.

Lila had prepared beef patties for hamburgers, and wrapped bacon slices around hot dogs to be seared over the open fire. There were platters of dill pickle slices, lettuce and tomatoes, and perfectly-sliced circles of sweet white onions. There were bowls of potato chips and assorted nuts, and squishy-soft hamburger and hotdog buns. And off to the side, sitting with regality, was a platter of fried apple pies—steaming, sweet fried apple pies, their pastry crusts shining in the early evening light.

We all ate dinner as we sat on lawn chairs set out by Mama, in a semi-circle around the roaring fire. After every single pie had been eaten and not a speck of food remained, Mama approached the fire from the house. She was carrying a large white box, holding it as far away from herself as she could, like it was filled with something vile: something so disturbing that only the destructive elements of a fire could destroy it. Then I noticed her hands. She was wearing a pair of white cotton gloves.

We all gathered around the intoxicating fire, and Mama placed the box on the parched ground. She lifted the top and pitched it into the fire, then invited everyone to don a pair of white cotton gloves so that only the gloves touched the contents of the box. We each took a position around the stark whiteness, and together watched it catch fire and begin to disintegrate. *Was that what was locked inside Mama and Daddy's closet last Christmas,* I wondered? And suddenly, I knew the answer. As the conical hat eerily charred, the image of three repetitive letters that had been seared in my mind like branded cattle ever since we found out what Daddy did began to dull and fade. Mama took up the bottom of the box and sent it on its crumbling path. She told everyone to remove their gloves and toss them into the flames, and I said, "Wait. Not yet."

I removed the white glove from my right hand and reached into the back pocket of my Levi's and brought out into the open the letter that Daddy had written to us.

"What is that, Lucy?" Mama asked.

"It's a letter from Daddy, Mama. He put it in the mail slot at Aunt Dodo's and Uncle Herman's when we went there after Christmas last year. It was written to me, Caroline, and Grace. We never showed it to you. We never showed it to anyone. And we don't want you to read it now. We don't want Grace to ever read it. We just want you to know that he wrote to us, apologizing for what he had done. He said that he loved us, and that he hoped we would one day forgive him. That day is today."

I slid my fingers back inside the white glove, and Caroline and I walked up to the fierce flames. We tossed the letter into the center of the fire together. We watched as the edges curled, charred, and turned to ash.

Mama had walked up behind us. She put an arm around each one of us and said, "I'm sorry. I'm so very sorry."

"That's okay, Mama," I said. "We know. It wasn't your fault. It wasn't anyone's fault. No one knew him, not even us. And he probably didn't even know himself." Suddenly, I was both amazed and quite satisfied at the depth of my own words.

We then each removed our gloves, creating a scattering of finality, and I felt someone take my hand, knowing that it was both familiar and unknown. I closed my eyes, and smiled up at the night sky.

# CHAPTER 38

Two days later, Daddy was dead. He had hanged himself in his jail cell with the belt from his trousers. He didn't leave a note. There was no funeral, but there was a front-page story in *The Commercial Appeal*. No one sent us a card. There were no flower deliveries to our house, either. No special foods were prepared and dropped off by friends and neighbors. We were all grateful, and yet our tears flowed as freely as if we had all aged gracefully, and watched Daddy play with his grandchildren on the veranda of the house we used to live in in Germantown. The only acknowledgement of Daddy's death was in that week's church bulletin: a single sentence at the very bottom read, "Pray for the soul of the father of Caroline and Lucy and Grace Moore."

Right before school started, we made a quick trip to St. Louis to place flowers at the gravesites of Aunt Dodo and Uncle Herman, who had passed away one week to the day after Daddy died.

Mama got a phone call from Mr. Zigler, their attorney. He said their house-keeper, Mrs. Plant, had found them when she arrived on a Tuesday morning, her usual cleaning day. She called out to them as she entered the kitchen, but no one answered. She called out again, gingerly walking through the kitchen to the front of the house. She found them wrapped in each other's arms, as if in a deep, sweet dream. They lay next to one another in the heavy four-poster bed that they shared, Uncle Herman's indigo patchwork crazy quilt from his childhood blanketing them both. She knew immediately that they had died, she said, because there was such a look of peace about them, a look that she had never seen before on anyone's face. It was time for them, too, to go home.

Mama was as sad as we'd ever seen her. We were, too. But all three of us knew that they, too, had changed. Through all the years of being a part of their lives, it happened that one winter season which seems now like a long time ago, that they did something none of us thought them capable of doing. They had taken down a wedding portrait, and with it our dreams and our futures. With one destructive blow, they had smashed in Daddy's face with a hammer, and they'd thrown the remains of it up in the attic. They too had thought what they did was right; yet in their hearts, in the end, they knew that it wasn't—just like Daddy. To each of us, it was almost as devastating as what Daddy had done. I guess no one ever really knows anyone—not completely.

WDM. HJR. KKK. MLK. Three initials, each set telling its own story. Separate, yet completely connected. Destructive and redeeming. It would be a very long time before I completely understood it, if I ever did. If any of us ever did. But one thing I knew for sure; we had all changed, and that would make all the difference in our lives, for the rest of our lives.

# CHAPTER 39

The past couple of months have been spent in a whirlwind, a hectic excitement in the air matching the crisp fall weather that sneaked its way through the normally still-warm early fall season in the South. It has been unusually cool, and we are told by friends of Mark's in West Virginia that it is even cooler in the Appalachian region, more so than usual "for this time of year."

We've never been to Appalachia before, and all I can think about are the pictures I've seen in my history books. The region is mountainous, of course, but also filled with deep valleys—and pockets of severe poverty. The people there are called Mountaineers, and all I can see in my mind is a burly, bearded man dressed in buckskin and carrying a musket. As it turns out, that's the mascot for West Virginia University—a university student dressed in buckskin, carrying a musket and wearing a coonskin cap. I can't get the black-and-white pictures from my history book out of my mind; they show a young mother who doesn't appear young at all, with three children seemingly attached to her legs, wearing tattered clothing and no shoes. Yet there is an instant familiarity; the porch of the house where they stand is in as much disrepair as the porch at our house on Stage Road. I was instantly linked to them in a most comfortable and uncomfortable way. I looked intently at their eyes, and they seemed to peer back at me with a warm welcome. I want to get to know them, to hear their story.

When I showed Mark the pictures of the different families and pointed out to him that they all looked identical to me in every way, he told me those families live in the hollows of West Virginia, and that I would likely not see that part of the county. "But I'd like to see that part of the county," I said with certainty. "I want to see all of it, not just the nice parts." He assured me that if that's what I wanted, then he would see that I traveled to all parts of West Virginia. I smiled, and he smiled back.

These families' faces look like they are dusted with a thin layer of coal. Coal is king in West Virginia. And the excavation of the coal from the mountain seams is very dangerous. First of all, I can't imagine what it would be like to work underground, with supports holding up the ceiling of the coal mine. In the pictures, the men's faces carry the same layer of fine coal dust, and they're bent over to keep from hitting their heads on the ceiling. I once tried to walk around the house in that position, trying to see what that would feel like. It didn't take me long to straighten up my back. I only walked around like that for a few minutes, and then I cringed at the thought of walking around like that for hours every day, like the coal miners.

Other photos were of coal processing plants along the riverbank. Mounds and mounds of coal were loaded into railroad cars and transported for use all over the country. But it was the other houses pictured in my history book that bothered me most. Houses that were just the opposite of the houses the coal miners' families lived in. They were grand; some were in the antebellum style, like the one we used to live in when we were in Germantown. These houses were owned by the coal company operators, the owners. They seldom went into the mines. I began to wonder why the men who went into the mines every day, their bodies hunched over for hours, praying that those supports would hold up that ceiling, had so little—while the owners had so much. It was a mystery to me, and I was anxious to find the answer, knowing that it wouldn't be an easy one to unearth.

The part of the state where we will live was once called "Death Valley." It was also referred to as "Chemical Valley." When I asked Mark about this, he told me that at one point in its history—which became even more scary and creepy to me as I learned about it—the area had the largest concentration of chemical plants in the country. The fifty-mile radius that ran from a place called Hawk's Nest (I like that name) west to Charleston was home to more chemical plants than anyplace else in the country. Years ago, there were very few environmental safeguards to prevent the emissions escaping from the gases that these companies released into the air, and the people in the area simply breathed it all in. In time, a lot of people became ill; many of them died. Eventually, laws were enacted to prevent those gases from permeating the air. I asked Mark if we would be safe there, and he assured me that we would, indeed, be safe. Still, I couldn't stop thinking about the history of this state. Its people seemed to wear the ravages of its wars on their sleeves. And again, I felt a connection to them.

I like the state's motto: *Montani semper liberi.* "Mountaineers Are Always Free." It suddenly occurs to me that none of us has been free for what feels like a very long time. We seemed to have been held captive in a world in which we had no part, and yet it continues to course through our veins slowly, without our even realizing it until we are forced to look at it—"like sands through an hourglass," one tiny grain after another.

As Mark tells me this story, which is so hard to understand, he sees that I am perplexed and changes the subject.

"I can't wait to take you to Hawk's Nest, especially the overlook there, which offers a panoramic view of the mountains, and the railroad, and the river. You can find all kinds of acorns, and half walnut shells, and twigs, and butterfly wings." And then he winks, and I know I'll love it, just because he is so certain. Mama winks too, and we talk about all the places we are going to visit before school starts. I get so excited that I can't remember what started the conversation. I am suddenly overcome with a childlike glee, and I can hardly wait to reach our destination. I can't wait to become a Mountaineer.

My biggest concern, though, is that the nearest public library is in the state's capitol, Charleston—an hour's drive from our home in Fayette County, an unincorporated town called Charlton Heights. There is no local law enforcement. It is just there, on its own. Free. But Mark has assured me that something called a Book Mobile will come to our little town every week. I like that idea—a vehicle that transports books and brings them to you. *As long as I can pull one from the shelf, open it, and bury my face in its ink-dappled pages, I'll be fine.* Mama says she will take me to the library in Charleston as often as she can, which is good enough for me.

Mark showed us a map of the valley, and it looks like someone turned over a can of worms. There are so many curvy lines, meandering rivers, and forested areas. Flat land appeared obsolete. Like the South, though, its humidity is high, and it sees lots of rainy days. I envision the rain forest, but I know the comparison is unrealistic. Still, I like to think I'll be living in a tree house of sorts, surrounded by pockets of bright sunlight, with creeks to wiggle my toes in; droplets of moisture from light rains that will tickle my eyelashes; and Sunday afternoon drives over steep, winding roads that lead nowhere and everywhere.

\* \* \*

As we drive through Charleston, I notice the state's capitol has a real gold dome, and as the sun begins its descent, there are pockets of the dome that are still blinding. I stare at it anyway, until it is out of view, until we are no longer on the interstate, driving along a two-lane highway called Route 60. One tiny, unincorporated town after another appears and then quickly disappears. Boomer (which I think is a funny name for a town), Alloy (where Mark will start his new job in a few weeks as a metallurgical engineer), Falls View (which doesn't have any falls to look at that I can see), and finally, Charlton Heights.

Turning off of Route 60, we head up a steep hill for what seems like forever, but which is only a couple of miles. We pass children on their bikes, people working in their gardens, and a big church with a magnificent stained-glass window depicting the Annunciation. We pass a house that has a tennis court, and another that has a trampoline in the front yard. When we get to the very top of the hill, Mama says, "There, on the left. The one with the dark green shutters. The white one. That's our new house, Lucy." It is beautiful. The lawn is the greenest green I've ever seen, and the front porch already has outdoor furniture on it. When we get out of the car, I notice a large wooded area just across the street from our house, with sounds from a babbling creek skipping over stones and gifts from nature that I've probably never seen before. I run to the back of the house. It is terraced, with a rose garden and a wall of glass from top to bottom and side to side. I peer through the windows, and it looks like something from one of Mama's decorating magazines. I am both thrilled and hesitant to walk inside. We are home, and that is all that really matters.

# CHAPTER 40

Shortly before we left for West Virginia, Mama took us with her to pick out her wedding suit. We went downtown, to Goldsmith's Department Store. We wore our very best clothes. Caroline dressed in a new Villager thin-wale corduroy chestnut-colored jumper, with a simple ecru turtleneck underneath, and brown cable-knit knee socks with penny loafers. I wore my navy bellbottoms with a Ladybug cherry red sweater set, one of my stickpins peeking out from the top button of the cardigan. My oxfords were shined to a high polish.

Before we began our shopping expedition, we lunched at the Tea Room, where we were served chamomile and lavender tea, accompanied by a three-tiered presentation of finger sandwiches (the thinly-sliced cucumber was my favorite); warm, flaky scones with clotted cream and strawberry preserves; and delectable, pastel-colored petit fours (I could have eaten a million of them).

After trying on many dresses of varying styles and colors, we all decided that she looked scrumptiously delicious in a very simple, yet elegant, soft celery green dupioni silk suit. The pencil skirt accentuated her delicate, model-like frame, and the long-sleeved, stand-up-collar bolero jacket featured a dyed-to-match narrow cotton lace trim at the collar and at the cuff of each sleeve. She chose a pair of light brown leather pumps, and a luxurious ecru silk chemise to wear under the jacket.

"Mama," Caroline said, "what type of jewelry will you wear?"

Without missing a beat she replied, "Well, I thought I might see if Lucy will let me borrow her pearl necklace. I think that will look lovely peeking out from inside my jacket collar. What do you think?"

"Precious," Caroline said. And for the first time that I could remember in a very long time, it was my turn to wink at them both, and smile like I hadn't smiled in what seemed to be an even longer time.

"That will be my 'something borrowed'," Mama said.

"What about the rest?" asked Caroline. "You still need something old, something new, and something blue."

"Well," Mama began, "my something new will be my wedding suit, and my something old will be my pearl earrings, and my something blue will be," and Mama said, without skipping a beat, "the sky."

Mama was the only person we knew who could say that the sky would be her something blue. She was always looking up, and knowing this about her made us slip into our new roles as easily as if that had been destined all along.

# CHAPTER 41

The morning Mama and Mark were married was cool enough to produce just a slight breeze, and the sun played hide-and-seek throughout the day. The sky was a robin's egg blue, and it was almost as stunning as Mama. It was a small, private ceremony, attended by the Andrews family and Lila. Mama looked almost regal in her new suit, and Mark cut a handsome figure in a light-weight woolen charcoal suit, starched white shirt, and hunter green tie with a design of tiny, interlocking navy squares. On her jacket, Mama wore a gold brooch in a floral design, with seed pearls. With Mark standing at nearly 6'6", Mama hit him perfectly just below his shoulders. But it was Grace who stole the show. She was dressed in a sweet little brown and light orange plaid taffeta dress, with a pinafore that matched Mama's celery-colored suit to near-perfection, which Lila had made for the occasion. And Lila was dressed in a light-weight navy blue rayon dress with a matching belt and tiny, shiny, red buttons that ran from the Peter Pan collar to the bottom hem. She carried a navy blue leather handbag, and wore navy blue cotton gloves. I had never seen the dress before, and she wore it with both pride and humility—not an easy task. Mama carried a small bouquet of gardenias, the scent of which would rival that of the honeysuckle blossom. And just maybe, in time, surpass it.

# CHAPTER 42

Mark sold his real estate holdings in the Memphis area, including the house we had lived in for almost five years. Since most of the furnishings were there when we moved in, we didn't have much to pack. We didn't need a moving van. Instead, we packed up the few personal items we had amassed, along with our clothes, and shipped them to West Virginia. Caroline had most of her things shipped to Morgantown, home of the West Virginia Mountaineers. She and Bernie had decided to room together after all, and Mr. Andrews tried hard not to smile whenever the subject was raised.

We said a tearful goodbye to Elizabeth and Diane. Petey and I spent the day before we left together, walking through the woods, holding hands, kissing, and pledging to stay in touch. He said the only thing he had to give me was his heart, and I said that was more than I deserved. He replied, "You deserve the very best, and that's my best." We picked up a few bird feathers and a tiny butterfly that was laying on the ground. Then he stopped and stared at something in front of us.

"What are you looking at?" I asked.

"Over there," and he pointed to something not two feet away.

"Where?"

"Just ahead," he said. "Come with me."

I walked with him to just before the yellow caution tape that was stretched around the dilapidated house that had once held Caroline's curiosity. It had been leveled some time ago, making way for a new Walgreen's.

Petey stooped to pick up a rather large wishbone that was resting on a stone. I had found many treasures on my haunts, but never a wishbone.

"Here," he said and handed it to me. "Put this in your Velveeta Cheese box," and we both laughed. I took it from him, wrapped both arms around his neck, and buried my face in his shoulder. He smelled of Aramis, the woods, and leather. I didn't want to let go. He nuzzled my neck and said, "Let's not make a wish. Let's wait until we see each other again before we break it." And I knew exactly what he meant.

# CHAPTER 43

I t seems that moving on was a good idea for many of us, however bittersweet it may have been. Lila, too. When we said good-bye, Mama asked her again to come with us. She had asked her many times, as had I, and Mark, and Caroline, and Grace—but the answer was always the same.

"Miz Maggie, you's startin' a new life. That gift is not given to many of us, but God has looked kindly on you, and you must look ahead. This is my home. It will always be my home. I cain't possibly leave it. I's comfortable here, and I's still got plenty to keep me busy. I loves you and your family, but I gots to stay, and yous got to leave."

When I hugged Lila good-bye, I couldn't have anymore let go on my own than if I was being promised the moon in return. It took Mama and Caroline both to unlock my hold on her waist. The sobbing shook every bone in my body. When my hold on her was released, she looked at me and said, "I loves you, Lucy Moore. Don't never change. Stay as lively and spirited as you've always been. Don't never let anybody tell you what's right and what's wrong, for you knows it yo'self. Yous can figure it out all by yo'self. In your soul, in the depths of your soul, you knows it, child. You's special. Don't you never forget it. You hear what I'm sayin'? Hold on to that. Never, ever let it go. You promise Lila now, ya hear? I wants to hear ya say that you promise."

Through my sobs, I said, "I promise. And I'll love you to the day I die."

"Me too, child. Me, too."

And she walked out of our lives as easily as she had walked into them. We were the ones who made it difficult. For her, it was always easy. And in time, I would realize that the reason it was so easy for her was because she knew she was special;

she knew what was right and what was wrong, for she was lively and spirited. She knew it in the depths of her soul, and she never forgot it. As she walked away from us forever, I handed her an envelope that held a single sheet of white paper, with a sketch of our honeysuckle vine that I had filled with soft watercolors and an acrostic poem that I had written for her.

## LILA

Like sands through the hourglass,
I keep each grain forever in my heart,
Leaving with you
Always my affection for teaching me what only you could have taught.

# CHAPTER 44

After we dropped off Caroline and helped her unpack her boxes, saying good-bye was harder than all the other good-byes had been. Bernie was not expected to arrive until the next day, so we had Caroline all to ourselves. There was so much to get done, keeping all of us busy, which left little time for tears to build. As she set out her things on her desk, organized and practical as always, I gave her a small package wrapped in chartreuse paper (not very easy to find) and a chocolate brown satin ribbon. When she opened it, she cried, which made me both happy and sad. It was seldom that Caroline ever cried, and even more seldom that she cried and was happy at the same time. She took the collection of Lady Bug stickpins and attached them to the ribbon before placing them on her desk. She then handed me a wrapped package, as well. My hands were shaking as I unwrapped the box. Inside was the Bailey Farms milk bottle that I had coveted for as long as I could remember. We hugged each other tighter than we ever had before, except for the time so long ago in Aunt Dodo's attic, when we found Mama and Daddy's mangled wedding portrait. It was a moment that I wanted to hold onto forever, but I knew that I had to let go.

"I love you, Lucy. I always have, and I always will. Even when we're not together, we'll still be together."

"I love you, too, Caroline. I loved you even before I ever knew you."

# CHAPTER 45

I t was a beautiful fall afternoon, with a light breeze and temperatures in the low 70s. The mountains enjoyed every color of green, from juniper, to emerald, to fern, and pine and seaweed. Mark put down the convertible top on the Buick, and Mama put on her floral, silk head scarf and her sunglasses. Indeed, she looked just like Barbie when I dressed her in *Open Road*. Mark looked just like Ken, in his denim bucket hat. I sat in the backseat with Grace, who wore her own sun hat, tied securely underneath her chin. She was giggling. I pulled my long hair back into a ponytail, then donned my shades and my new WVU Mountaineers ball cap, bringing my ponytail through its open back.

We pulled into McDonald's drive-through and ordered a Coca-Cola and some fries before we started our journey over the mountains. As we made our way through the hills and valleys of the Appalachian region, I knew that we had left so much behind. Yet I knew that so many others were traveling with us: Petey, Lila, Thomas, Albert, and even Daddy. They were all a part of us and always would be, no matter how much we might like to rid ourselves of some of the memories. And unless we held on to all of them, we would never be who we were destined to become.

As I looked around and noticed our new surroundings—the winding roads, the lush forests, and the hills dotted with houses and people and dogs—and began to wonder at the magic those mountains held for us, I was gently and convincingly reminded by everyone who had touched my life to not only look into someone's eyes, but to see. Really see. And suddenly, the sun's rays seemed to shine brightest on what was closest.

# ACKNOWLEDGEMENTS

Many years ago, after reading a very early draft of *Honeysuckle Holiday*, Peggy Fox with New Directions met with me when I attended the Sewanee Writers' Conference and wrote: "You captured the voice of the twelve-year-old girl very well." It was that single sentence written to me in a typed letter that remained a constant source of encouragement for me throughout the writing of the novel.

To my first "real reader," my niece, Natalie Grace Widmer, for offering valuable suggestions, reminding me to "leave something for the reader to figure out for themselves"—thank you.

To my friend, Barbara Byrge, who read the book, not only with an astute reader's eye, but also with the precision of an expert proofreader and the gentle nudge to "give me more." My sincere gratitude.

To Brian Hoskinson, IT consultant extraordinaire, whose unending patience in helping me "present" the book to the world through technology, my deep appreciation. And somewhere along the way, he became a rather astute editor.

To my Goddaughter, Leah Tuckwiller, who read the book when she and it were both so very young.

To my dear friend, fellow writer, and brilliant student Anna Muehlman Hartman who read the manuscript more times than either of us is willing to count, offering suggestions on everything from storyline to dialogue and creating the perfect cover art for the book. I am humbled by your support and encouragement. You are the one person whose love of TKAM just might surpass my own. An engaging student turned remarkable teacher.

To my sister Cynthia Jones, who always makes certain that my feet are planted firmly on the ground and my sister Melinda Widmer, who always encourages me to fly–thank you both.

To Janie Jessee of Jan-Carol Publishing and her editorial staff–many thanks.

And finally, to John, without whose constant encouragement this book would have never been written. I am deeply grateful for much more than your keen editorial eye. Thank you for completely believing (long before I did) that I could write this story. And thank you for every line-by-line critique you gifted with the objectivity that isn't easy to inject after growing up together for the past forty years. You are life's true nectar.

# ABOUT THE AUTHOR

Kathleen M. Jacobs's work has appeared in regional and national publications. She holds a Master of Arts degree in Humanistic Studies, and has taught English and Creative Writing on the high school and college levels. She divides her time between the Appalachian region and New York City. *Honeysuckle Holiday* is her first young adult novel.

CPSIA information can be obtained
at www.ICGtesting.com
Printed in the USA
FFOW03n2340280318
46012199-46910FF